UP IN FLAMES

Rafferty and Llewellyn Titles by Geraldine Evans

ABSOLUTE POISON *
DEAD BEFORE MORNING
DOWN AMONG THE DEAD MEN
DEATH LINE
THE HANGING TREE

* *available from Severn House*

UP IN FLAMES

Geraldine Evans

This first world edition published in Great Britain 2003 by
SEVERN HOUSE PUBLISHERS LTD of
9–15 High Street, Sutton, Surrey SM1 1DF.
This first world edition published in the USA 2004 by
SEVERN HOUSE PUBLISHERS INC of
595 Madison Avenue, New York, N.Y. 10022.

British Library Cataloguing in Publication Data

Evans, Geraldine
    Up in flames
    1.   Police - Fiction
    2.   Murder investigation - Fiction
    3.   East Indians - Great Britain - Fiction
    4.   Detective and mystery stories
    I.   Title
    823.9'14 [F]

    ISBN 0-7278-6034-8

Typeset by Hewer Text Ltd.,
Edinburgh, Scotland.
Printed and bound in Great Britain by
MPG Books Ltd., Bodmin, Cornwall.

Flames

The blue idol in the corner of the room was untouched by the fire. While delicate fingers held the silver flute to his lips, his painted eyes gazed down on the twitching form of the young woman on the floor. The once shapely limbs were now blackened. The glorious fall of silky dark hair was now a rusty stubble.

As the idol watched, flames began to caress the bright cartoon transfers on the white-painted cot. Above the snuffed-out whimpers of the deeply sleeping infant could be heard the distant clanging of fire engines.

The fire flickered up the curtains. More hungry now, the tongue of flame licked across the ceiling. Molten plaster dropped on to the figure on the floor. The young woman's body lifted slightly, gave what sounded like a sigh, then settled and lay still.

Through it all, the flute-playing idol played on, his sweet, silent music a poignant serenade.

One

The fire had been quickly extinguished. The neighbours, who had been evacuated by the firemen, had been allowed to return to their homes by the time DCI 'Will' Casey's car with DS Thomas Catt at the wheel, edged its way forward.

The row of small Victorian terraced houses was situated in a narrow side road on the outskirts of the eastern market town of King's Langley, and the fire brigade vehicles were lined up in the middle of it. With the area car parked across the road behind the fire engines they could drive no further. Catt pulled up and parked neatly beside the police car. As they climbed out, they silently took in the chaotic scene.

Beyond the firemen in their bright yellow helmets, milling around as they stowed their gear, Casey caught a glimpse of the uniformed officers from the area car. They were keeping the crowd of neighbourhood onlookers herded out of the way at the far end of the street. The hoses from the brigade's vehicles writhed like snakes across the pavement, ready to trip the unwary. Great puddles lay in front of the blackened ruin in the middle of the terrace. Incongruously, the puddles reflected only the brilliant blue of the August sky.

Casey straightened the jacket of his plain, sombre-hued suit as he gave a tiny approving nod. The scene might look chaotic, but it was an organized chaos. Beneath the surface confusion, Casey recognized the quiet competence of well-oiled routine. What a pity it had been in vain.

Gus Freeman, the assistant divisional fire officer, approached them. Soot streaked rakishly across his cheek,

3

giving him a piratical air, but under the grime his normally cheerful face was strained.

'Chief.' After exchanging the brief greeting, Casey got straight to the point. 'I gather you've got two bodies?'

Freeman nodded. 'One adult. One infant. Asians, according to the neighbour.'

Casey's green eyes shadowed at this news. He offered up a little prayer that this latest fire proved accidental. But after the recent spate of arson attacks on local Asian families, he wasn't optimistic. He steeled himself and voiced the question he had been worrying at since he'd first heard about the latest fire. 'Was it arson?'

The arson attacks had caused a furore in the town. Fortunately, until now there had been no fatalities. Anxiety had made Casey's question come out sharply, but the fire chief didn't take offence. They had come to respect one another. Even though Casey, at thirty-five, was ten years younger than the fire chief – and with his quiet, unconsciously puritan air and immaculate dark suit he was in stark contrast to the large, normally ebullient and slightly scruffy chief – the pair got on well.

'Arson's a possibility,' Freeman admitted. 'One of the neighbours, a Mrs Angela Neerey from number 7a, next door but one to the scene, told me she smelt petrol shortly before she noticed the neighbour's flat was on fire, but as her neighbour on the other side made a habit of topping up his petrol tank from a can in the street, she thought no more about it. Even when she smelt the smoke she just assumed it was another neighbour having one of their regular barbecues.'

Beside Casey, Thomas Catt murmured, 'The normal scents of summer in suburbia.'

'Exactly. That's what Mrs Neerey thought. It was only when she got up to go into her flat to top up her drink that she noticed the neighbouring flat was on fire. That's when she rang nine-nine-nine. We've only just got the fire out, so have had little time to check for other signs.'

'She didn't notice anyone suspicious hanging around?' Casey asked.

Gus Freeman shook his head. 'She was sunbathing in the back garden.' He went on to say that, according to the neighbour, a young Asian girl by the name of Mrs Chandra Bansi lived there alone with her baby daughter.

Casey stared grimly at the smoke-blacked ruin. Briefly he wondered why an Asian girl would live alone with her baby. It was unusual. The Asian way was the extended family all living together. He asked Freeman, 'Notice any sign of a break-in?'

'None that I could see. But the back door was only a cheap wooden job. Mrs Neerey was fairly certain the back door was shut when she first went out into her garden, and was still shut when she noticed the fire. The lock wasn't good quality either and was so twisted from the heat that it was impossible to tell if it was locked or not. Apart from that, I saw nothing to indicate that it had been forced, certainly no chisel or other marks, though admittedly, as most of the wood had burned away, I couldn't swear to it. The front door was locked and still intact when we arrived. It was a better quality door. We had to smash it down to gain access for our hoses.'

Casey nodded and asked the question that could no longer be avoided. 'Where are the bodies?'

'Ground floor. Back living room. There's access from the rear as there's an alleyway running along the entire row. I've notified my control. They're sending out a team of fire investigators.'

The police team were also on their way; the scene of crime team, photographer, forensic and Dr Arthur Merriman, the pathologist. Casey knew Dr Merriman, for one, was likely to be some time as he lived and was based nearly twenty miles away. But meanwhile there was plenty to be getting on with. 'What about the top flat?'

'Empty, luckily. A repossession job.'

'I want to have a look at the scene. Has the structure been made safe?'

'It looks worse than it is. There seems to be little structural damage. But get hard hats in case of falling debris, and masks as there might be some lingering toxic fumes.' He gestured at the poorly maintained row of terraces. 'The area's run-down, so I expect the soft furnishings were second-hand and stuffed with the old-type foam.' Grimly, he joked, 'We don't want any more fatalities.'

The SOCOs and the brigade's fire investigators arrived simultaneously. Casey and the fire chief walked over together as they got their equipment from the vans parked one behind the other at the rear of the fire engines. The narrow street was beginning to resemble a gridlocked race track. After he and the chief had briefed the SOCOs and fire control teams, Casey thanked Gus Freeman and left them to it.

He and Catt approached the police officers keeping the crowd back, and Casey asked them, 'What can you tell me? Have you had a chance to speak to any of the other neighbours yet?'

PC Jonathon Keane, the area driver, shook his head. 'Me and John Jones had our hands full just keeping the gawpers back out of harm's way.'

'OK. I'll get others on to that.' He went on briskly, 'I want you to get a clipboard and make sure you get the name of everyone that enters the house from the front. Find someone to do the same from the rear.' After the firemen had clumped through with their equipment, Casey realized this was probably a waste of time. But if this turned out to be arson it was essential he did everything by the book in case an investigation followed. 'But before you do that, find some more bodies to help Jones keep that crowd back out of the way. Send someone to let me know when the pathologist gets here. Once I've looked at the scene I'll probably be with the neighbour, Mrs Neerey at 7a.'

After directing other officers to search for any discarded container with petrol or other accelerant dregs, Casey and Sergeant Catt climbed into their white protective gear and borrowed hard hats and masks from the brigade vehicle. They made their way round to the alleyway that Gus Freeman had mentioned.

The fire had blasted the windows out and the grass in the back garden glittered diamond-like in the bright sunshine. Treading carefully over the grass's slippery carpet, they approached the house. Casey checked inside the back door for glass, but there was nothing to point to an intruder. It was all outside, making walking treacherous. Although the back door was badly burned away by the fire, Casey, like the fire chief, couldn't see any obvious marks to suggest a forced entry, and remarked as much to Catt.

'But it's a warm day,' Catt pointed out. 'I know Mrs Neerey *thought* it had been shut, but after seeing her neighbour's home ablaze she'd have been in shock and could easily have been mistaken. But either way, we don't know if it was locked, which is more to the point. If it wasn't, anyone could have gained easy access from the alleyway.'

Having checked the exterior, they approached the window of the living room and peered through the now black and jagged frame.

The body of the adult was lying in the middle of the floor and, as is often the case in a fire, it had adopted the typical 'pugilistic attitude', with the arms extended and the forearms flexed in a boxer's pose. The legs, too, were flexed. This stiffening, Casey knew from previous conversations with the pathologist, was caused by the coagulation of the muscles on the flexor surface of the limbs. But to Casey it suggested that the victim had fought the fire and suffered the inevitable, painful defeat. There was an infant's cot near the window and he could see the tiny, blackened form through the metal bars. It, too, had adopted a boxer's stance.

He closed his eyes and took a few deep breaths. Behind him he heard the crunch of glass as the rest of the SOCO team entered from the back alley. He opened his eyes and, from a throat suddenly raw with held-back emotion, said, 'Let's leave them to it. I want to speak to this neighbour, Mrs Neerey, anyway.'

They carefully retraced their steps and headed for 7a. Mrs Angela Neerey, tear-steaked and obviously distressed, was standing in her doorway, watching the comings and goings and shaking her head. She was a fair-haired woman in her early thirties with a wide, generous mouth that looked as if it would smile readily. But now, its full curves were compressed. Her eyes were puffy, and she had a tight grip on the handkerchief in her right hand. Her gaze fixed steadily on Casey and Catt as they walked up the path.

'Mrs Neerey?' Casey asked. She gave a quick nod. He introduced himself and Catt.

'You've found them?' she questioned, in a tear-thickened voice.

She must have watched as they spoke to the fire chief and guessed the worst, Casey surmised. 'Two bodies have been found,' he quietly confirmed. 'One a baby. But I'm afraid we'll have to wait for positive IDs.'

Mrs Neerey paled as she took in the implications of this. She swallowed hard, blinking rapidly to keep back further tears. And as she crumpled the handkerchief tightly in her fist, she asked, 'Was it . . . was it an accident or . . . or another arson attack?'

'We don't know for sure either way yet,' Casey told her, hoping to deflect her questions. But she persisted.

'You must have an idea.'

Cautiously, Casey told her that arson was a possibility.

Her generous mouth tightened. 'Then for God's sake make sure you catch them this time. We don't want anyone else getting away with murder. We don't want more riots.'

Her harsh words were a brief foretaste of what Casey knew he could expect if this *did* turn out to be arson. He glanced at Catt, but the normally upbeat, even cocky ThomCatt was subdued and unnaturally silent. That, more than anything – even the, so far, brief view of the victims – brought home to Casey what kind of task lay in front of them.

And after the uproar that had followed the failed investigation of black teenager Stephen Lawrence's murder in south London, Casey knew that if his worst fears were realized and this *did* turn out to be arson, the emotions that had been running high in the town since the first Asian arson were likely to explode.

Slow-fused and patient beyond most men's capacity, Casey suspected both traits would be tested to the limit. And not just by the Asian community . . .

Two

A minute later they were in Mrs Neerey's sunny kitchen at the back of the flat. Decorated in shades of yellow and white, it should have looked fresh and clean. But smoke from the fire had laid a coating of grime over everything.

'Please, sit down.' She gestured at the cheap pine table and four matching ladder-back chairs placed just under the window. After quickly wiping the chairs with a duster, she picked up a couple of toy trucks that lay on the floor in their path. 'My son's. He's asleep, thank God. I was just making tea. Would you like some?'

'Please.' As they sat and Catt took out his notebook, Casey told her, 'It's really more for background information on your neighbour. Though, of course, we'll need to go over everything you told the fire chief.'

The tea was made, poured and brought to the table. Mrs Neerey sat down opposite Casey.

'If I can just confirm your neighbour's name?'

'Chandra. Chandra Bansi, and Leela was the baby's name.' With a catch in her voice, she added, 'Nine months old and just getting to that interesting stage.' Her lips tightened as she grappled with further tears. 'She and my little boy used to play together. What am I going to tell him?'

Confronted with such an impossible question, Casey could do nothing but awkwardly shake his head. 'And Mrs Bansi– Chandra – how old was she, do you know?' he asked when she had blown her nose and taken a sip of her tea.

'She was twenty. I know because she had a birthday last

Friday and she invited me in for a glass of wine. She's only lived here a few weeks.' She gave a bleak smile and dabbed her eyes. 'I suppose you think it's foolish of me to be so upset over such a short acquaintance.'

Casey shook his head. 'Such a death would upset anybody. And with the baby, too . . .'

Angela Neerey nodded, sniffed, then resumed her story. 'I liked her, you see. I believed I'd got to know her in the time she was here. I felt sorry for her as she seems to have had a terribly thin time of it lately.'

'In what way?' Casey questioned.

'In what way hasn't she is more to the point. For instance, you know she was recently widowed?'

Casey shook his head again. 'At the moment, I'm a blank canvas. Anything you can tell us will be helpful.'

'As I said, she was a widow. A very recent widow. Her husband only died a month or so ago, though from what she told me I don't think Chandra was too broken-up about it.' She hesitated. 'It sounds awful to be talking about her in this way when she's just died and in such a horrible way, but I got the distinct impression she regretted her marriage. I gather Magan, her husband, was the jealous type, possessive, besotted even. You can imagine that didn't endear her to her mother-in-law, who I gather thought her son's love for Chandra was not only turning him into a fool, but turning him against his mother. Well, she was a beautiful girl and of course it was an arranged marriage. As usual in such a marriage, she'd lived with her in-laws, and I gather that hadn't been a very happy experience.' Her lips pulled back in a grimace. 'It's not much fun living with in-laws, as I know only too well. They chucked her out, you know, when her husband died. Blamed her for his death.'

Casey glanced at Catt before he asked, 'You've no idea why?'

She gave a tiny shrug. 'Only-son-syndrome, I imagine. No one would have been good enough. And then Chandra was very westernized and had decided opinions of her own. I gather that didn't go down too well, either.'

'You seem to have learned a lot about her in a few short weeks.' Casey gave one of his rare smiles. A slight lift to the corner of his mouth, a crinkling warmth to the eye, then it was gone. It was almost as if he had a limited supply of such smiles and that this supply might be exhausted at any moment. Perhaps he had. In these politically correct times the average copper has little reason to smile. And Casey, with the prospect of conducting what was likely to prove a difficult investigation in the full glare of critical publicity, had less reason than most.

Angela Neerey managed a tremulous smile in return. 'We had a bit more than one glass of wine on her birthday, as it happens. That's when most of this came pouring out. And it helped, I suppose, that we're both in the same boat. Both on our own, with babies, I mean. We babysat for each other. Chandra was a bit reserved, but friendly. God knows, she had her troubles. But she was just a normal young woman. That's why . . .' she broke off, unable to continue.

Not quite normal, Casey reminded himself as he thought again that it was far from normal for a young Asian woman to live alone with her baby. He asked Mrs Neerey about it, but she was able to tell them little.

'I found it curious myself,' she told them. 'I asked her about it once. It's not as if she was on bad terms with her family. Her parents came round a couple of times. It all seemed perfectly amicable. On the surface, anyway, though I noticed none of her family ever babysat. Not even her grandmother, who you would think would love to spend time with the baby as she's only over for a visit. But then Chandra did say her nan hadn't been well. Though, to be honest, I wondered whether that might not be an excuse.'

'Why would she need one?' Catt asked.

Angela Neerey pulled a rueful face. 'Little Leela was a bawler, I'm afraid. I had to grit my teeth when I minded her, but I used to feel so sorry for Chandra, having to cope alone with a baby that never stopped crying, that I did it anyway just to give her a break. I'm lucky. I've been blessed with a good baby, but the boot could so easily have been on the other foot. I did wonder whether Chandra, given the predicament she found herself in, didn't feel any resentment that her parents pressed her into the marriage. It would be a natural reaction, as I gathered that Chandra only gave in and agreed to the match when she was depressed after failing her exams. The implication being that she wasn't bright enough for a career and that it made more sense for her to get herself a promising husband. Anyway, between one thing and another, she gave in and agreed to marry her father's choice.'

'And had ample time to regret it ever since?' Catt commented.

'That's about the size of it.' She sighed. 'I suppose that's partly why I'm so upset about all this.' She waved a hand in the direction of her young neighbour's ruined home. 'I think Chandra was trying to find the courage to make a fresh start, to break away from her family and their expectations of her. Maybe even study for a career. She certainly had the courage to try. Now she'll never have the chance.'

'What about her family, Mrs Neerey?' Casey asked quietly. 'Do you know where they live? Or their surname?'

She shook her head. 'Call me Angela, please. Though Chandra did mention that her father was a businessman and owned a string of clothes shops.' She screwed up her face in an effort to recall. 'I seem to remember her mentioning that one of his shops is on the High Street. I believe the flat she lived in was his, too.'

Casey gestured to Catt and he went out into the hall with his mobile. One of the first priorities would be to get positive IDs on the victims. With luck, from the information Angela Neerey had given them, plus dental records, Chandra Bansi, at least – if indeed it was she lying dead in the flat – should be quickly identified. Hopefully the forensic investigation of the fire and the post-mortems on the bodies would reveal whether the two victims had been killed in the fire, or had already been dead and the fire started in an attempt to conceal their murder.

Suicide, given what Angela Neerey had told them, was, of course, another possibility, although death by self-immolation was rare. And then there was the baby; a mother would surely not put her child through such a death. But the fact that she had lived in the flat for such a short time was a point against arson; at least, anything other than a random arson. She could hardly have lived there long enough to have made enemies.

But it was pointless speculating at this stage. The time for that would be when they had some evidence to speculate with.

Casey's musings were interrupted by Catt's return. He gave a brief nod to confirm that Mrs Neerey's information had checked out.

Angela Neerey had become quiet and they sipped their tea in a reflective, companionable silence. Casey, enjoying this lull before the storm, lifted his gaze to the back garden. It was a warm day with a clear blue sky. The back door was open. A fresh breeze fluttered the flimsy yellow and white gingham curtains and wafted the smell of smoke into the room. From here, he could see the abandoned sun lounger. A pair of cheap sunglasses had been discarded a few feet from the lounger, a bright-blue plastic glass lay on its side a few yards closer to the house, presumably dropped by Mrs Neerey when she realized her neighbour's home was ablaze.

Although small, the garden was well stocked and a kaleidoscope of colour and pattern met his eye. Generous swathes of bright yellowy-orange rudbeckia with its rich, hot chocolate-coloured centre, fiery orange Crocosmia with its branching stems, white and mauve love-in-a-mist and many more were crammed into the limited space. Their fresh beauty struck a harsh contrast with the sight two doors down of charred bodies, twisted metal and blackened walls.

Casey turned back to Angela Neerey. 'Did you hear anything from next door? Screams or cries? I understand you were in your garden when you first noticed the fire.'

She shook her head and cupped her hands round her now cooling tea. 'Unfortunately, I had my headphones on,' she explained. 'I was listening to rock music. I like my rock good and loud.'

It was Saturday lunchtime – surely some of the neighbours would be at home. Casey hoped one of the other neighbours might have heard something. With the weather so warm there would be open windows and doors, so any noises or cries would be easily audible. It was now nearly 2 p.m. Mrs Neerey had reported the fire around one o'clock. Conscious of the passing time, and all that had yet to be accomplished, Casey pressed on. 'Tell me, was Chandra security conscious?'

Angela Neerey nodded. 'Yes. So am I. Let's face it, a woman alone is an easy target. And after the local arson cases, being Asian, she must have felt even more vulnerable. That's why I'm surprised her father put her in the flat when her in-laws threw her out instead of taking her back home.'

So was Casey.

Thinking about the victims' Asian background prompted him to ask, 'Do Chandra's parents speak English?' Obviously Chandra did, but she was of the younger generation. Often the middle-aged and elderly Asians kept to their own people and had little occasion to speak English.

'Her father seems to. Of course, I've done little more than passed the time of day with him, but he understood my collo-quialisms well enough. I don't know about his wife, though. She just smiled and nodded on the couple of occasions they visited. I don't even know their names. As I said, Chandra only lived there a few weeks, so I had little time to discover more.'

She seemed to have discovered most of Chandra's short life history in the brief time she had known her, Casey reflected. And if this should turn out to be more than an accident and more than a random arson, it might be fortunate for the investigation.

He heard a rapid rat-a-tat. Casey leaned over and gazed up the hallway. PC Keane stood at the open front door. He called down the hallway. 'The pathologist's here, sir.'

Casey nodded, thanked Mrs Neerey for her help and handed her his card. 'If you think of anything more, please ring me.'

Dr Arthur Merriman, the pathologist, was the complete antithesis of his name; A Merry Man he was not. Thin, severe and not at all given to the telling of jokes – macabre or any other kind – he was just getting into his protective gear as they approached his car.

Casey and Catt, who had stripped off their protectives before they spoke to Angela Neerey, quickly climbed back into them. 'It's like a war zone in there,' Casey warned the pathologist. 'Better get a helmet.'

After borrowing another hard hat from the fire crew, Casey led the way through the smashed front door of number 5a and gestured Dr Merriman ahead of them towards the back room.

As the pathologist stood on the threshold of the room studying the damage, Andy Simmonds, one of the forensic team, called over to Casey. 'That looks the most likely seat of the fire,' he said and pointed to an area of charred floorboards in the middle of the room. Apart from the adult's corpse and clumps of plaster, the area was bare of articles that might have started the fire. 'Curious,' was Simmonds' comment. 'Unless we've got a case of spontaneous combustion . . .' He nodded around him. 'You can see the progress of the fire across the room.'

Casey took his word for it. The room didn't speak to him as it obviously did to Simmonds.

'If this does turn out to be arson, I'd check out the local hospitals.' Simmonds went on, 'Arson can be a hazardous business – and not just for the intended victims.'

'What do you mean?' Casey asked.

'Petrol evaporates at a very low temperature, so if there was a delay between setting an accelerant and lighting it, enough vapour can rise to create an oxygen-petroleum mixture that explodes – a fireball. Any arsonist may have sustained burns to their hands and face. The local casualty departments could provide a rich source of suspects.'

Casey thanked him for the tip and added, 'I'll get it checked out.'

Dr Merriman had approached the first body while Casey and Andy Simmonds were talking. Without comment, he studied the corpse of the adult where it lay on its back, a couple of feet or so away from the area Andy had said was the likely centre of the fire. The body was covered in chunks of plaster from the ceiling.

The room looked even more desolate from the inside. Water from the firemen's hoses still dripped down the blackened walls. What remained of the furniture was just springs and bars, the metal had twisted and contorted till, to the imaginative, each piece looked like a strange crouching beast, skeletal and sad.

Catt, seeing the still strangely undamaged blue idol in the corner, nodded at it and commented, 'Must be a god of fire, naturally protected from flames.'

Casey didn't correct him. But, as he had reason to know, the Hindu god of fire was Agni. And although he had lost his usual peacock feathers, Casey recognized him as Krishna; the many-faceted Hindu god, and while his many followers were particularly passionate, fire didn't come under his sway. If he remembered rightly, the festival celebrating his birth was around this time of year.

The SOCOs in their hard hats and masks were still busy, collecting their various samples. Every so often one of them would call out to the civilian photographer to get a shot of something. Since the spate of local arson attacks, Casey was becoming sadly familiar with the routine.

Dr Merriman beckoned them forward. Casey and Catt moved gingerly, trying to disturb as little as possible.

'Fierce blaze.' As usual, the pathologist got straight to the point. He spared little time for social pleasantries. His thin, dry voice revealed no emotion as he added, 'The adult has sixth degree burns. The infant, from the little I have so far observed, seems to have been burned to a lesser degree.'

Casey knew this was the highest category of burn. He could see that the skin tissue and muscles were mostly destroyed, with the damage extending to the large blood vessels and bones. And as he stooped over the body on the floor he noticed the trauma to the skull. 'Looks like she was bludgeoned.'

Dr Merriman, as always, was non-committal. But his voice took on that irritating lecturing tone that Casey knew so well. 'Such injuries can be caused by fire. Intense heat, such as occurred here, can subject the soft tissue to splitting. The skull is particularly vulnerable to such damage as the bone is so closely underlying the skin.' In an aside presumably not intended to sound macabre but nonetheless managing to make Casey's skin crawl, he added, 'I've seen corpses where the heat build-up in the head causes the skull to explode.'

Casey grimaced. Catt, too, looked a bit green. He pulled a face as they exchanged glances. The pathologist went on to tell them that, as usual, any definitive answers would have to wait till the post-mortems.

Dr Merriman directed the photographer to take more pictures of the cadaver on the floor. Just then, Casey and Catt were called away by Constable Anderson, one of the uniformed officers he had directed to search for discarded accelerant containers.

As he led them through the rear entrance and out of the back gate, Anderson told them, 'We've found a vacuum flask chucked amongst the rubbish in the alleyway. It still contains a small amount of what smells like petrol.'

Something positive, thought Casey as he quickened his step. 'You didn't touch it?' he questioned.

Anderson shook his head. 'No, sir. Besides, I had my gloves

on.' The young officer held white-gloved hands in the air as if looking for approval.

Casey nodded. 'Good man. Get a photographer and one of the fingerprint team here.' As Anderson hurried away, Casey lowered his head and sniffed the contents of the red vacuum flask where it lay nestled within the open folds of a black plastic bin liner. His nostrils flared as he caught the distinctive and pungent odour of petrol.

Three

After the flask had been shot and tested for prints, it was bagged and tagged ready to be sent to the lab.

Casey commented quietly to Catt, 'With Mrs Neerey's claim that she smelt petrol shortly before she noticed the fire, plus Andy Simmonds' conclusions, this is the clincher. Our arsonist is now a double murderer.'

Casey told a hovering Anderson to contact Sergeant Imry at the station and get an incident room set up. 'And find a few spare bodies and start a house-to-house. Someone must have seen something.'

Casey paused for several seconds after the young officer, speaking into his shoulder radio, had hurried away up the alley. He gazed up at the warm, blue sky with its few cumulus clouds wafted by the soft breeze. His nostrils flared as he sniffed the air. The light breeze had changed direction and was blowing the smoke from the fire away from them, towards the centre of town. It smelled fresh and clean now, faintly scented with lavender – no doubt from Angela Neerey's well-stocked garden. He sighed, then asked sadly, 'What sort of person can set out, on such a day as this, armed with petrol to deliberately, callously, wantonly destroy two young lives? What kind of creature could decide to kill on a day that should make you think only of the joys of life and its free and simple pleasures?'

Catt glanced up at Casey's set face, noted the sooty-lashed eyes were at their most vivid green and attempted an answer. 'Somebody mad. Somebody bad. Somebody dangerous to know.'

'Perhaps whoever did this was all three.' Casey paused for a few seconds to absorb the horror. 'While we've got a minute, tell me. I gather you managed to obtain the details of the victims' family?'

Catt nodded. 'The father's name is Mr Rathi Khan. His wife's Savitri Khan. They live about half a mile from here, in Great Langley.'

'Anything known about the family?'

'No. But Angela Neerey was right about the father owning a chain of shops. The clothes shop on the High Street *is* one of his. I rang the main office and Mr Khan is working in the High Street shop this afternoon.'

Casey nodded. 'Let's get over there. If Mrs Neerey is right and the flat is one of his properties, it's possible the arson was intended for him rather than the daughter. He must be a successful businessman, from what Angela Neerey said. Maybe someone had a grudge against him. No one becomes successful without stepping on a few toes.'

'Unless he torched it himself.'

Thomas Catt had a habit of jumping to cynical conclusions; unfortunate given the possible racist implications of the case. But as long as ThomCatt kept such remarks between the two of them, Casey was prepared to consider them. At this early stage he would be foolish not to consider every possibility. 'Insurance job, you mean? A businessman who's not as successful as he would like the world to think?'

Catt nodded, brought out the comb which he seemed to carry everywhere and smoothed the slickly styled hair that the fireman's helmet had ruffled. It was how he had earned his nickname. ThomCatt was as particular as the most vain Persian cat about personal grooming. 'Maybe, after the other arson cases, he thought it would be timely to jump on the bandwagon.'

'With his daughter and baby granddaughter inside? Too cynical, even for you, ThomCatt. And put that comb away, for the love of God.' The puritan in Casey was uncomfortable with his sergeant's obsessive grooming habits. 'This is a murder scene, not a barber's shop.'

An orphan, who had been abandoned as a toddler and brought up in a succession of children's homes, Thomas Catt might well feel the need to adopt a well-cared-for image, but he usually had a short way with family sentiment. He lived alone in a streamlined bachelor flat through which an endless succession of girlfriends came and went. Catt had never shown signs of getting serious about any one of them, to Casey a sure sign of his sergeant's fear of commitment; scarcely surprising given his background.

Now Catt shrugged, put his comb away and commented, 'Maybe he expected them to be out. Maybe he hired a couple of thugs who didn't trouble to check before they torched the place.'

'Either way, it's early days yet. Later, it might be necessary to discreetly check out his financial situation, find out if he was in debt and desperate for funds. But let's wait and see. Maybe we'll learn something from his reaction when we break the news. I'll want to speak to the mother as well.'

Remembering Angela Neerey's comment about the mother possibly not speaking English, he told Catt to get hold of Shazia Singh, the one Asian WPC the station possessed. 'We might need her when we speak to the mother. Maybe for the father as well. Even if he speaks English well, if it's his second language shock might make him temporarily forget it. We'll pick up Constable Singh from the station. Just hope she speaks the same language as the family or we'll have to wait while another translator is found.'

Casey was anxious to extend every consideration right from the start; something he was always careful to do with every bereaved family. But Superintendent Brown-Smith would certainly insist that this case demanded extra-sensitive handling, particularly after the Stephen Lawrence investigation and the damning report that followed.

'While you're organizing that I'll see if Dr Merriman and forensics can tell us anything more yet.'

They walked in companionable silence to the end of the alleyway so as not to get under the SOCOs' feet more than necessary. They had reached the gate of number 5a, and Casey said, 'Wait for me here when you've arranged for Shazia Singh. I doubt I'll be long.'

While Catt got on to the station to arrange about the Asian WPC, Casey banged his hard hat back on his sternly barbered dark head and adjusted his mask before he re-entered the crime scene.

The SOCO team were still hard at work, Dr Merriman still working on the adult corpse. After a quiet word with the forensic investigators, he got Casey's help to turn the body over.

Although the victim's back showed signs of burns, they were mostly only first or second degree. There were patches of skin that were barely touched by the fire. Dr Merriman bent over and examined them, pointing out the cherry-red colour of the skin to Casey. It was the colour skin – and blood – took on after carbon monoxide poisoning and told them the adult, at least, had still been alive when the fire started.

Casey stood back. A muscle in his cheek tapped out a staccato rythmn as he studied the charred cot and its pathetic contents. 'The baby, too, I suppose,' he muttered, more to himself than Merriman.

'All in good time. You should know by now that I prefer to concentrate on one corpse at a time. The infant will receive my attention in due course. And as I do not go in for guesswork . . .'

Barely aware he had spoken, Casey glanced at him in surprise. But he should have known better than to utter such a question within Merriman's hearing and he made no further comment.

The pathologist and the rest of the team were obviously going to be here some time yet, so Casey told the pathologist he was leaving the scene. 'Going to break the news to the family.'

The pathologist didn't bother to raise his head, but unbent enough to comment, 'An unpleasant task. Fortunately for me, the dead have done with heavy emotions.' He added an admonition, 'Don't forget to ask who the victim's dentist was. We'll need forensic orthodontics for this one.'

Casey, well used to Merriman's unnecessary instructions, said nothing and went out. Before picking up Catt, he had a word with the house-to-house team. But they had, as yet, discovered nothing more. The neighbours claimed to have heard no screams or cries.

Casey took this information with a pinch of salt. Given the circumstances of the two deaths it seemed unlikely the young woman and her baby hadn't screamed. Unless the damage to the adult's head *had* been caused by a blunt instrument, rather than the fire. But the post-mortem would provide the answer to that question. Anyway, as Chief Freeman had observed, it was a run-down neighbourhood. Screams, even in the middle of the day, were possibly too common an occurrence for anyone to pay them any heed.

Still, disappointed at the lack of hard information, he walked back to pick up Catt and break the news to the victims' family.

After they had extricated their car from the logjam of vehicles still clogging the narrow road, Casey and Catt drove to the High Street.

Parking was always a problem in the centre of town. King's Langley was an ancient market town in the eastern half of England, equidistant from Norwich and Peterborough. Medieval in original, it was full of crooked streets and crooked houses with half-timbering and jutting upper storeys that looked prettily quaint but blocked out the light.

To the modern motorist the town was as exasperating as it was pretty, as its streets were even narrower than the Victorian Ainsley Terrance on the town's outskirts, where Chandra Bansi's flat was situated.

Catt dropped Casey and WPC Shazia Singh outside Rathi Khan's clothes shop. And as the shop was housed in one of the quainter buildings in a road barely wide enough to allow a single vehicle passage, Catt had to drive off to find somewhere to park.

Outside, the shop rails held the usual assortment of Western clothes: dresses, skirts, blouses, shirts and trousers, mostly coloured, modern and drab. But inside, the shop was alive with enough colour and scent to intoxicate the senses. Brightly coloured silks and cottons cascaded from grey oak beams. They made a startling, vivid contrast to the plain simplicity of whitewashed plaster and half-timbering and made the store look a particularly alluring Aladdin's Cave of jewel-bright treasures.

As Shazia Singh spoke quietly to the female assistant, who disappeared into the back recesses of the shop after darting one curious glance at Casey, he gazed around him. And as he took in the familiar, brilliant colours of India and smelled the sandalwood perfuming the air, he was immediately transported back to his childhood.

Inevitably, thoughts of India brought his parents to mind. He had been very young, of course, when they had brought him on the hippie trail to India, like many others before and since, following in the path The Beatles had trod before them. He had been dragged all over the country on their wanderings. Even now, he could still recall the smells of exotic spices as well as the other, less exotic and equally pungent aromas brought by inadequate or non-existent drainage coupled with stifling heat. He had caught malaria. It still troubled him occasionally. He had come to hate the place.

Of course, his parents had loved it, so they had all stayed for months. His mother had even adopted the wearing of saris and salwar kameez, in her element in the colourful crowded bazaars. She had gone a long way to becoming more Indian

25

than the Indians. A peculiar role reversal when it was Asians in England who were often said to be trying to out-English the English.

Nowadays, in an England grown coarse, with their politeness and courtesy Asian immigrants *were* more English than the English, many of whom had forgotten or never learned the good manners of previous generations.

Briefly, he wondered how his parents were. The smallholding on which they lived had no telephone. And although Casey had bought them a succession of mobiles, they always either lost them or never bothered to switch them on. Certainly, they rarely rang him. But although that no longer either surprised or upset him, they were still a perpetual worry. He hadn't seen them for some time and the thought made him uneasy. He resolved to somehow find time to drive out to their smallholding buried deep in the Fens to see how they were getting on.

With a sigh, he thrust these personal anxieties to the back of his mind and forced himself back to the here and now. It struck him that Rathi Khan seemed to be taking an inordinately long time to come the short distance from the back of the store. While they continued to wait, Casey did some more studying of his surroundings.

The age and style of the building didn't readily lend itself to clothes retail. It was cramped, with unexpected steps which raised the floor level for no apparent reason that Casey could see. Unless the medieval mind that had designed the row thought it a good wheeze to twist ankles and rick backs.

Mr Khan had made an attempt to meet the old building halfway. Instead of the expected modern shop counter, there was an ancient sideboard. A modern till sat incongruously on its grey age-patinated surface. Dotted around the shop were old wooden settles which, by their colour, were of a similar vintage to the sideboard. With high backs and ornate carvings, their seats were piled high with more glowing bales of silk and cotton and richly embroidered brocades. He thought how much his mother would enjoy this place, rummaging for bargains. Perhaps she could still even manage to speak a bit of Hindi; she had picked up a fair smattering during their time in India.

Catt returned from parking the car a second or two before the assistant finally emerged from the rear of the shop followed by a smartly dressed Asian man. Chandra's father. Rathi Khan was a man in his mid to late forties. Tall, and light-skinned for an Asian, his features were aquiline, finely sculpted, and he carried himself with an air of unconscious dignity. He paled noticeably after Casey had introduced himself, Shazia Singh and Sergeant Catt.

He confirmed he was the owner of 5a Ainsley Terrace. He seemed hesitant and nervous. Casey, tainted, in spite of himself, by ThomCatt's cynical suspicions about a possible insurance fraud, wondered why that should be when he had yet to disclose the reason for their visit. But, he told himself, it was probably just the immigrant's natural anxiety when having dealings with the police. Besides, it was only to be expected that he should be concerned that something had happened to his daughter and grandchild.

Even so, it was odd in a businessman who had done well enough to own a string of shops. And since Tony Blair had brought in the full panoply of the Human Rights Act, Casey thought it unlikely that a presumably educated immigrant like Rathi Khan shouldn't be fully aware of his rights. Surely he should be demanding answers rather than meekly waiting for them to be supplied?

Casey encouraged Mr Khan to sit down on one of the settles before breaking the grim news. He watched him closely, but all he saw was the natural reactions to shock – disbelief, denial, then a dawning realization of the horror of what he was being told. The man looked sick to his soul.

So much for Catt's cynical suspicions. Casey would reserve judgement till they had something firmer than will-o'-the-wisp theories on which to base their conclusions.

Once the initial shock had passed, Mr Khan became very quiet. Although he was aware that people's behaviour after bad news could go from dumb at one extreme to voluble at the other, Casey wondered whether there might not be something else behind the silence. But time and the continuing investigation would hopefully reveal that something – if it existed at all. For now, as Casey reminded himself, all they knew for certain was that the man had lost his daughter and granddaughter in a particularly horrific way and was bereaved.

Gently, Casey asked Mr Khan for the name of his daughter's dentist. This simple request dragged Mr Khan from his silent reverie and he was able to supply the information without more than a second's hesitation.

'We'll need photographs of your daughter and the baby.' Casey paused before adding, 'And we'll need to break the news to your wife, of course.'

This seemed to release something pent-up in Mr Khan's soul, for he launched into an incomprehensible stream of some sing-song Asian language. Again the memories stirred in Casey's mind. But he had no time for them now. He glanced at WPC Singh and she nodded to indicate that she could understand. It was a relief to discover she spoke the same language as the family.

Rathi Khan's torrent of speech ended as abruptly as it had begun. Now his expression again became closed. When Casey asked if he would like Sergeant Catt to drive his car back to his house, he looked momentarily blank, asked, 'What?' before understanding dawned. He nodded and began to dig in his trouser pockets for the keys. Once found, he absently separated his car keys from the house keys and handed them over to Catt. But before he did so, Casey had time to notice another set of keys on the ring, poignantly marked 'Flat – front door' and 'Flat – back door.' Doubtless they were spares to Chandra's flat.

'My car's in the yard behind the shop. The yellow Yale is the key to the gate.'

It took a while to get Mr Khan sufficiently together to get him out to Casey's car. Even though the day was warm, he insisted on going back for his jacket and putting it on. He said not a word during the short journey to his family home at Great Langley.

The house was impressive. Located in an expensive area where the neighbours would be doctors, lawyers and other successful businessmen, as he pulled up and parked away from the garage so as to leave room for Catt to put Mr Khan's car away, Casey gained a quick impression of the house. The house gave the lie to Catt's suspicions. There could be no shortage of money here, surely? A large family house, it was detached, imposing Edwardian in style, though obviously built fairly recently, with all of the attractions of that era, but none of the expensive maintenance that an old building required. It was a practical compromise. The house stood in its own grounds, and a circular gravel drive enclosed a bricked bed of mixed, low-growing, easy-maintenance evergreens.

They got out of the car and Casey guided Mr Khan's now shaky steps to the front door. Casey heard the sound of a child's laughter inside the house as Rathi Khan fumbled with his keys. Casey took them and opened the door, ushering the man ahead of him into the hallway. As they entered, Casey heard a car's tyres scrunch on the gravel behind him. It was Thomas Catt at the wheel of Mr Khan's Rover.

Having seen the house and learned of the chain of shops, Casey was surprised that Rathi Khan drove a four-year-old Rover. He would have expected something more recent and top of the range.

It was the first indication that Catt, with his natural cynicism about human nature, might be right and that Mr Khan might not be as comfortably placed as the large house suggested. Maybe there *were* money troubles here. Thom-Catt's cynicism was contagious, Casey realized as he found himself thinking again of Catt's earlier suggestion that he look into Mr Khan's finances.

A child, a little boy of two or three, ran towards them as Casey walked into the hall. The boy threw himself at Mr Khan's legs with excited squeals. A grandson, Casey guessed. And from his bright, eager chatter and smiles, the way he hugged Mr Khan's legs and tried to clamber into his arms, it was apparent that he was a much-loved child.

Obedient to the toddler's demands, Mr Khan picked him up, burying his face in the child's chubby neck as he did so. The little boy continued to chatter away in Hindi, but when he got no response he grabbed Mr Khan's ears, pushed his head away from him and began what sounded like an imperious scolding. Mr Khan still said nothing, but merely deposited the child on the floor and called loudly down the empty hallway.

Casey broke the awkward silence. Hunkering down on his haunches till he was at the little boy's level, he said, 'Hello. I'm Will. What's your name?'

Shyly the little boy put his thumb in his mouth and stared.

Behind him, Shazia Singh broke into a musical flow of Hindi. The little boy mumbled something in reply that Casey couldn't catch.

'He's called Kedar, sir.'

Casey nodded. 'Where's your grandmother, Kedar? We need to speak to her. I'm afraid your grandad's had some bad news.'

The little boy turned and pointed down the hall. A plump, middle-aged woman appeared at the far end. Dressed in a pale sari, she must have heard the commotion for she stood transfixed and stared at them all, one hand tightly clutching the material of her sari, the other covering her mouth as if to stop herself crying out. Above the clutching hand, her eyes were wide and anxious; the red bindi dot on her forehead stood out starkly against the unnaturally waxen skin. Her anxious pallor was natural enough, Casey supposed, in an Asian woman, on finding her home invaded by strange white men and a uniformed Asian policewoman. As he recalled, the bindi dot was supposed to signify female energy and was

30

meant to protect a woman and her husband. This dot had failed in both departments.

Still, taken together with her husband's earlier behaviour, he wondered whether there might be something more here than the immigrant's natural mistrust of the police. Wary now, again remembering Catt's cynical evaluation, he stood up.

Four

Upset by the suddenly tense atmosphere, the little boy's face puckered and he began to cry. Perhaps for the first time in the child's life, neither of his grandparents attempted to comfort him and it was left to Shazia Singh to gather him in her arms, produce a tissue and try to wipe his tears away.

Raising his voice over the child's sobbing, Casey quickly introduced himself, Catt and Shazia Singh to Mrs Khan. 'Perhaps we could all sit down?' he suggested to Rathi Khan.

Before he could say more, Mr Khan brushed past him, grabbed his wife by her forearms and told her, in English, 'Chandra is dead. And the baby. They were in a fire at the flat.'

Her hand clutched even more tightly at the gathered folds of her sari as she stared at her husband. Casey half expected her to collapse, which was why he had been keen for them to be seated before he broke the news to her. But Rathi Khan had forestalled him. Mrs Khan appeared dazed as she stared up at her tall husband. And no wonder, was Casey's thought. As a breaker of bad news, Rathi Khan was in a class of his own. He was certainly no waster of words or sentiment.

'A fire?' Mrs Khan repeated, in a voice that was oddly expressionless. 'They are dead? My Chandra and little Leela?'

Rathi Khan nodded and took his wife's arm. 'Come. Let us sit down as the inspector suggests. He will tell us more about what has happened.' Distraught, he spoke to Casey in Hindi. '*Kshama kijiye*,' it sounded like, which Casey seemed to remember was a form of apology, before he collected himself and, with a formal politeness, said in English, 'Please to come in.' He led the way across the wide, high-arched hallway to a large and comfortable room with a double aspect to front and rear. Light flooded into the room from the large windows, bathing the room in afternoon sunshine.

Comfortably furnished with three pale yellow sofas grouped around the empty fireplace, with chintz-covered armchairs scattered in companionable pairs in between, the room revealed little of the origins of its owners. Unlike Chandra's flat, her parents' living room had no idol watching over its inhabitants. It seemed to lack ornaments of any sort. Clean, functional, comfortable, but curiously anonymous, it was as if its occupants were merely passing through.

An elderly couple were seated in two of the armchairs. Chandra's grandparents over from India on a visit, Casey guessed. The man clutched an Asian-language newspaper. He stood up, still clutching his paper, as they entered.

Rathi Khan introduced them. 'My father and mother, Mr and Mrs Ranjit Khan. They're here on a visit from their home in India.' He broke the bad news quietly in English.

The old man took it stoically, with all the fatalism of India. Tall like his son, and bony, with heavily furrowed features, Casey guessed he was in his late sixties; a generation clearly used to sudden bereavement. His wife remained seated. She had been engaged in cleaning the household brass. It was the first homely touch Casey had observed in the characterless room and, as her gloved hands continued desultorily with her cleaning, he guessed that she spoke little or no English and didn't understand the reason for the upset; certainly no one had troubled to explain to her what had happened. But although her cleaning continued automatically, her bewildered gaze flickered from face to face. The bindi dot she wore was much larger than her daughter-in-law's, almost like a third eye. Casey found it oddly disconcerting to be the focus for this unblinking red orb.

Perhaps intimidated by such a sudden flurry of visitors, Mrs

Khan senior said nothing. But an Asian woman of her generation would have had plenty of practice in keeping her opinions to herself, Casey guessed. He remembered Angela Neerey's comment that Chandra's gran hadn't been well and he wondered whether the grandmother, who couldn't be any older than her late fifties or early sixties and who looked in reasonable shape, hadn't invented her ill health to get out of babysitting duties with the ever-bawling Leela.

After one furrowed glance at his wife – as if worried she wouldn't share his stoicism – Ranjit Khan insisted on shaking the hands of the two policemen. He ignored Shazia Singh, much as his wife, after several more troubled glances, ignored them and went quietly back to her slow rubbing. Presumably, she had been well trained from an early age not to intrude on men's business.

All the conversation so far had been conducted in English, a language it was clear the old lady didn't speak. It seemed cruel to keep her in ignorance, but if she truly wasn't well, Casey didn't want to be the unwitting cause of even more upset. Maybe it was best that her son break the news to her after they left. And given Rathi Khan's none too gentle way with bad news, Casey thought it might be kinder if he, Catt and Shazia Singh didn't form an audience.

Although it was a warm day, the windows were closed. Presumably this was for the grandmother's benefit, as the old lady's sari was overladen with several thick shawls and a chunky buttoned cardigan. And as he remembered the sweltering heat during parts of the year in India, Casey guessed she felt cold even on what English natives would consider to be a perfect summer's day.

Once they were all seated, the Rathi Khans on one of the long yellow sofas, Catt, Shazia Singh and himself on assorted chintz armchairs, Casey explained as gently as he could that it didn't look like an accidental fire.

Chandra's mother stared at him. 'Not . . . not accident?'

Her husband waved her question aside as if in reminder

that, as the man of the house, it was for him to do the questioning. She subsided meekly enough, but the glance she darted from under her lowered lashes held something more than meekness. 'What then? Arson, do you mean?'

Casey nodded. 'It looks that way. Had your daughter received threats of any kind? Had she upset anyone recently?'

Rathi Khan started to shake his head, then stopped and gazed thoughtfully at him as if the connection had just occurred to him. 'You're thinking of those other arson attacks on local Asian families, are you not, Inspector? You think someone did . . . that, to my daughter and the baby?' Mr Khan glanced worriedly at his wife and mother and back to Casey.

'It seems a possibility,' Casey admitted. 'That's why I need to know as much about her life as you can tell me. *Did* anyone threaten her?'

Mr Khan hesitated, then said slowly, 'Chandra did mention something. Two white youths hassled her only last week outside the flat. She was putting the rubbish out. Called her – well, the usual racist nastiness. My Chandra is . . . *was*,' bleakly, he corrected himself, 'a spirited girl. She never meekly accepted abuse from anyone, even when it might be more sensible to say nothing. She told me she called them a pair of ignorant idiots and that they should go back to school and learn some manners.'

'Did they assault her?'

'She said one of them tried to grab her arm, but she was too quick for them and got the gate between them and her. Told them that if they didn't go away she would call the police. After shouting more obscenities, they left.' He shrugged. 'That was all there was to it.' His troubled gaze met Casey's. 'Do you think they might have done this dreadful thing?'

'We don't know, Mr Khan. It's early days. Tell me, when exactly did this exchange between your daughter and these youths take place?'

He frowned as he thought back. 'It was on Thursday morning. Just a couple of days ago.'

Today was Saturday. A short enough time for any of her neighbours who had observed the youths to remember their behaviour. 'Did your daughter describe them to you?' He shrugged. 'Skinhead yobs is all she said. These aggressive, shaven-headed youths all look so alike, don't they? Do you think they could have come back and set the fire? From such little provocation?'

It was Casey's turn to shrug. 'We can't rule anything out at this stage, Mr Khan. Obviously, we'll speak to your daughter's neighbours. See if any of them saw these skinheads. We might get a fuller description. It's possible they're known if they're local.'

The little boy's chatter broke in to the pause in their conversation. He was standing by Shazia Singh's knee and had obviously taken to her. He had raised the sleeve of his shirt and displayed a bandaged arm with all the pride of a wounded warrior as he chatted in Hindi.

His grandmother called to him, quite sharply, 'Kedar, come here. Not to bother the police lady.'

Although Shazia told her the child was no trouble, Kedar's grandmother was insistent. Obediently Kedar went and perched on her lap. Once settled, he lost interest in everything but his bandage and gazed at it with a pleased smile on his otherwise serious little face.

Rathi Khan's mother suddenly paused in her desultory brass rubbing and spoke to her son in Hindi; softly at first and then with a growing sound of demand as he apparently tried to evade her questions. He must finally have given in and broken the news to her because her hands flew to her face. She let out a terrible wail, stood up and staggered. The brass ornaments she had been cleaning crashed to the floor at her feet, creating an appalling cacophany that set Casey's teeth on edge.

Rathi Khan caught his mother and half carried her back to her chair. She collapsed into it, tearless as yet, but with a lost, hollow look in her eyes, she began to chant the names of her granddaughter and the baby over and over again.

'My mother is not well,' Rathi told them quietly as Mrs Khan's cries upset the little boy and started him sobbing all over again. 'It is best she doesn't know all the details. I have told her only that they are dead. It is enough. For now, at least.'

His mother plucked at his sleeve. Her voice had turned querulous; even Casey caught the note of reproach although he failed to understand the Hindi. With a glance of apology to his visitors, Rathi Khan excused himself and half dragged, half carried his mother from the room.

He returned after five minutes. 'I have given her a sleeping pill,' he told them. 'It is better that she sleeps. She might bear her grief more calmly after a rest.' He sighed softly, gazed at his quietly weeping wife and grandson and observed, 'No amount of weeping will bring them back.'

He had called his son from Casey's mobile during the drive from the shop and now, as Casey heard another car pull up on the forecourt, he guessed it was the son. He glanced out of the window and saw a sharply suited Asian man in his midtwenties slam the car door and hurry to the entrance. Footsteps approached the door, and after a single glance that took in the little tableau of police, parents and grandfather, he crossed immediately to his mother and embraced her.

'My son, Devdan,' Mr Khan explained by way of introduction.

Apart from saying, 'Dan,' in correction of his father, in what seemed to have become an automatic anglicized adoption, the younger man simply nodded in acknowledgement of their presence, but said nothing. He was a good-looking young man, with a straight, classically sculpted nose, firm lips now tightly pressed, and highly planed cheekbones. Tall, with his father's features and light skin, he carried himself well. His plentiful hair blow-dried in a sleek style, he looked modern, totally English in a way his parents would never be. He sat on the other side of his mother, lifted the little boy from her lap on to his own and took the hand that still had a death grip on the material of her sari. Casey began his questioning again.

'I understand that your daughter and her baby lived alone. Isn't that a little unusual?'

Rathi Khan's hand gripped his wife's other hand more tightly as he told Casey, 'It was a temporary arrangement only. Just until I could organize something better. My daughter was recently widowed,' he explained. 'Naturally, I wanted her back home with her family, but we are bursting at the seams here at the moment. As you see, I have my mother and father over from India on an extended visit; my son, his wife and two small children, as well as my younger daughter and my wife and myself, all living here. The house may look large, but it still has only four bedrooms.'

Casey nodded, but he still thought it odd that room couldn't have been found for the widowed Chandra and her baby. How much space did one young woman and a small baby take up, after all? But then, as he recalled all the paraphernalia that expectant colleagues had bought in preparation for a new infant, he thought Mr Khan might have a point. Even so, and especially given the series of local arson attacks, it seemed foolhardy for him to have left his daughter alone in a flat in a run-down part of town.

He wondered where the son's wife and the younger daughter and granddaughter were. They must be out or all the commotion would surely have brought them running. 'I understand that Chandra had only lived at the flat for a short time – you own it, I believe you said, Mr Khan?'

'Yes. It is my flat. Of course, until her husband died, my daughter lived with her in-laws.'

At this, the son burst into a sudden torrent of Hindi. His father waved his hand at him and glanced at Shazia Singh as if to remind him of her presence. He seemed to be doing his best to shut his son up. But the son shook his head vehemently, turned to Casey and in unaccented English told him, 'My sister's in-laws threw her and the baby out of the house. She—'

'It is not necessary to tell the police this,' his father broke in. 'It is not relevant and—'

'Why should we keep it secret?' Devdan Khan demanded. 'It is their shame, not ours.' Devdan – or Dan, as he seemed to prefer to be called, overrode his father's objection and turned back to Casey. 'My sister had not borne a son, you see. She was a disappointment to them. And then, when Magan, their son and Chandra's husband, died, they blamed my sister.'

Casey sat forward. Although he had already learned this from Chandra's neighbour, it was as well to get the more intimate, family version. 'Why was that?' he asked. Was it possible that Chandra and the baby had died as a result of a family feud? Such things weren't unknown. It seemed that one of her family, at least, might suspect such a possibility.

'It was nothing.' Rathi Khan broke in again. 'It was just that they were distraught, grieving. My son is too young yet to understand that the pain of bereavement can make people hasty and unthinking.'

'I, too, am grieving,' Dan pointed out to his father. 'Their grief is no excuse for what they did.' He turned back to Casey. 'Chandra and her husband had had an argument the day before he died and—'

'My daughter could be a little wilful,' Rathi told them. He sighed. 'It is the Western influence. She was too outspoken for a young woman.'

'Anyway,' Dan broke in. 'Her husband wanted to make up, so to please her, he gave her money to buy new clothes for herself and the baby. He dropped her and Leela at the shops. He had an accident on the way back.' He paused, then added, 'A fatal accident. Her in-laws blamed my sister. When they arrived back home from the hospital, Mrs Bansi, her mother-in-law, began to scream at Chandra. Told her she had brought bad karma to their family.' He sighed. 'All the usual religious mumbo-jumbo was used as an excuse. Anyway, they threw her out, her and the little one. Told her she should take herself to Varanasi or Vrindavan and try to behave like a dutiful sorrowing widow.' He broke off to explain to Casey and Catt, 'They are two towns in India where unwanted widows go to live out the rest of their days mourning their husbands.' His voice thickened as he added, 'Chandra and Leela would still be alive if it wasn't for their cruelty. She would have been safe at their house, not alone and vulnerable at the flat.'

Was that the closest any of the family would come to an accusation? Casey wondered. He also wondered why Rathi Khan was so keen to play it down. Perhaps it was a generation thing? Or perhaps, as well as the marital connection there were also business connections between the two families. Asian families tended to tie interwoven threads of kinship. No doubt he was concerned that he might suffer business loss on top of his personal bereavement. Was he, in that fatalistic Indian way, saying that life must go on? It wouldn't help this practical aim if his son spread his anger amongst the wider Asian community. Besides, at this stage there was no evidence to point the finger at Chandra's in-laws. Anyway, hadn't Dan Khan said that his sister would have been *safe* if she had remained at the home of her in-laws? The use of such a word scarcely implied that he suspected them of being the cause of Chandra's death.

But it was for him to investigate this and every other possibility. And as there would never be a better time than now, while they were unguarded and outspoken in their grief, to discover if there was any such evidence, Casey probed a little deeper. 'So there was bad feeling between your families?'

Dan Khan shrugged. 'They had been saying unkind things about Chandra. Untrue things. Making all kinds of accusations. They even—'

'That is enough, Devdan,' his father insisted. 'What's done is done. It was their grief talking, I am saying, nothing more. Like your poor sister, it would be more seemly if you kept a respectful tongue in your head, my son. Remember to whom you are talking.'

From Dan's silent but simmering expression, Casey guessed

he would get no more information. At least, not in the presence of Rathi Khan. Now he changed the subject and asked Mr Khan, 'Was Chandra security conscious?'

'It is these skinhead yobs you are thinking of, yes?'

Casey, wary of being pushed on to one particular track, said cautiously, 'The skinheads are one possibility. But they're not the only ones. There were no obvious signs of a forced entry, you see.'

Rathi Khan nodded absently at this, as if it was something he had expected. 'I told her she must keep the doors and windows locked. She said she would.' He shrugged. 'But the young are careless about such things. Maybe she was slapdash and with the warm weather . . .' His explanation tailed off, then he added, 'Of course, if she left the back door or windows open or unlocked anyone at all could have got in. Is that what you are thinking happened, Inspector?'

Casey nodded. 'It seems a likely possibility. I'll need to speak to your daughter's in-laws. Could you let me have their address and full names?'

'What for do you want to speak to them?' Rathi Khan asked anxiously. 'I told you they can have had nothing to do with this business. They are decent, honest merchants, no matter what my son may say.'

His son didn't seem keen for them to pursue the matter either, only his reasons were rather different. 'They will only poison your mind against Chandra,' he told them. Suddenly, he seemed to be backtracking. Casey wondered why and what Chandra's in-laws might reveal.

'I will, of course, bear that possibility in mind, sir,' Casey reassured him. 'But I am investigating the cause of your sister's death and that of her baby, not her character.'

They both fell silent at this, as if they had each remembered their mutual grief and felt rebuked. Casey was relieved that neither of them thought to challenge his assertion. But, as with all murder victims, the unfortunate Chandra *and* her character would get as thoroughly investigated as the crime itself.

Mrs Rathi Khan broke in and spoke to her son. Devdan gave a brief reply and she asked Casey in broken English, 'Why? Why you see them?' She turned to her husband and spoke to him in Hindi.

He gave her as brief an answer as had her son.

'Does your wife understand much English?' Casey asked.

Rathi Khan hesitated before he replied. Perhaps he hoped to shield his wife from the distress of their questions. Or perhaps, as Catt would no doubt believe, he didn't want anyone else but himself to provide answers.

'My wife understands a little only. But more than she speaks. She mixes rarely outside our own community. Like my son, she is upset because she fears Chandra's in-laws will speak badly about her to you. And not just to you, to the Asian community also.'

'What my father means is that what they say will reflect on our family.' The son sounded bitter. 'My father has not only a good business within our community, he also has the future of his younger daughter to think of.'

'You, too, have a daughter you will need to find a husband for some day,' Rathi Khan quickly reminded his son. 'Besides,' he appealed to Casey, 'is it wrong to want the best for a child? It is too late now for Chandra. But I want my younger daughter to have her chance to marry well.' He gave a tiny lift of the shoulders. 'Such things are important. Bad blood between us and Chandra's in-laws, Mr and Mrs Bansi, will not help the situation.'

Casey gave an understanding nod, and with yet more quiet persistance Mr Khan was persuaded to supply the details of Chandra's in-laws. There was little more to say and Casey rose, satisfied that they had two possibilities to check out – the skinhead yobs who had harassed Chandra, and her grieving, unkind parents-in-law.

He asked Mr Khan if the family would like Shazia Singh to stay with them to give what comfort she could, but his offer was refused.

'We are better alone,' Mr Khan told them, adding, with a glance at his son as though issuing a reminder, 'We are a private family.'

'We'll leave you in peace then. If we could just have that photograph of Chandra and one of the baby.'

Mr Khan went to the large and ornate marble fireplace that dominated the room, picked up a silver-framed picture from the mantelpiece and handed it to Casey. 'That is my Chandra. My beautiful Chandra. As you can see, Leela was just like her.' He gave a sad, fleeting smile. 'Though only like her in beauty. Chandra was always such a good baby. Leela was what I believe you English call a bawler. Always she cried, that child.' His face shadowed. 'Perhaps, even so young, she sensed her fate.'

Embarrassed by such a mawkish sentiment and the raw pain behind it, Casey concentrated on removing the picture from its frame, taking rather longer over the job than it strictly required. Wordlessly, he handed the frame back and dropped his gaze to the photograph.

Chandra *had* been a beautiful girl, with long, lustrous midnight-black hair and pale, luminescently clear skin. The spirit that her father had mentioned earlier was evident in the laughing dark eyes that stared boldly out of the picture. This was no shy, reserved Asian girl. Chandra looked like she would be capable of giving her mother-in-law as good as she got.

As he studied the picture of the young and undeniably beautiful Chandra and her equally beautiful, doe-eyed baby, Casey was suddenly filled with melancholy, saddened that all the youth, beauty and vitality evident in the photograph should now be lying charred and ruined in the mortuary. For in her photo, Chandra looked so wonderfully, vividly alive as to make death, particularly such a death as this, all but unbearable.

Conscious that he was intruding on a grief he had no right to share, Casey told them, in a voice roughened by emotion, 'I'm sorry for your loss.'

Rathi Khan nodded and clutched his wife's hands more tightly. '*Shukriya.* Thank you. You . . . you will keep us informed?'

'Of course.' Casey glanced again at the photograph. 'I promise you I will find whoever committed this dreadful crime.'

Rathi Khan met his gaze. He said simply, 'I'm sure you will, Inspector.' His bleak expression only emphasized the fact that this wouldn't bring back his laughing, beautiful daughter or her baby.

Before Casey had the opportunity to leave, the front door slammed again. The sound of laughter echoed down the hallway and a young Asian woman in her early twenties and two girls of around four and thirteen came into the room. The woman and the teenager clutched a variety of colourful carrier bags and, judging by the quantity of bags and the pleased expressions, had evidently had a successful shopping trip. They stopped abruptly as they saw Casey, Catt and the uniformed WPC.

'What is it? What has happened?' The young woman asked Devdan.

Devdan ignored her and it was left to his father to briefly introduce them, 'Rani, my daughter-in-law and Kamala, my second daughter.' He paused, then added poignantly, 'Who is now my first.'

'First?' For a moment, the teenager looked merely puzzled, then anxiety spread across her pretty face. It was easy to see she was Chandra's sister. Her sister-in-law, with her blotchy skin and heavy features, looked very plain beside her. 'What do you mean, Dad? What has Chandra done now?'

Her words revealed her assumption that her parents, rather than life itself, had disowned Chandra. Rathi Khan waved a silencing hand at her. 'She has done nothing. Of course, she has done nothing. But we have had some bad news. Some very bad news about your sister and the baby.'

'Tell me.' Young Kamala stood, with clenched fists, in the

middle of the room, tension radiating from every pretty facial contour.

Her father told her, more gently than he had his wife, but not gently enough. There was no gentle way to tell such news, after all. Kamala burst into tears and threw herself at her mother. Rani Khan, Devdan's wife, also began to cry and turned to her husband for comfort, but he brushed her aside, picked up his little girl, and kissed her tears away instead, leaving his wife standing forlorn, sad-eyed and ignored.

Casey felt uncomfortable, but his training hadn't deserted him. His observation told him that young Kamala's grief was real enough. But Rani's? Casey wondered whether he had imagined the look of satisfaction that had momentarily pinked and prettied her plain face before the tears flowed. Had her husband noticed it, too? Or was Devdan's careless attitude merely habitual?

As Kamala's agonized weeping hiccuped to a close, Casey felt sure he hadn't imagined the betraying expression. But if Rani Khan had felt no great liking for her beautiful sister-in-law, what plain woman would? Chandra had been adored by her own husband and loved also by her brother, her sister-in-law's husband. And poor Rani, standing alone and still uncomforted, appeared to be loved by no one at all. Even her children preferred to be comforted by others. With Chandra dead she had one less rival for her distant husband's affections. Anyway, judging by the quantity of shopping bags, she had been otherwise occupied during the relevant time and could have had nothing to do with Chandra's death.

From where she sat, encircled by her mother's plump, bare arms, Kamala suddenly burst out at her father, startling Casey as much as anyone. 'Why did you have to stop me from visiting Chandra at the flat? Now I will never see her again.'

Her words seemed to catch her father on the raw. He looked defenceless, his face a stiff death's head of grief. It seemed as much as he could do to mutter, 'I told you. Chandra needed to be alone. She had just lost her husband and needed to consider her future. She didn't need your thoughtless chatter upsetting and distracting her.'

The answer didn't satisfy his younger daughter. With all the passion of youth, she wrenched herself from her mother's embrace and stalked to the centre of the room to confront her father. 'Come on, Dad. Don't pretend that Chandra was in deep mourning for Magan. The last time I saw her was at his funeral and she seemed dry-eyed enough then. But that doesn't mean that she wasn't lonely, especially after the way those Bansis treated her. But no, we left her all alone in that dreary flat. You, who are all the time going on about the strength of the family. Where were we when she needed her family the most? You wouldn't let me babysit. You wouldn't even let Mum or Gran babysit and I still don't understand why.'

Kamala was tall, nearly as tall as her father. Rathi Khan seemed to shrink as if intimidated by this thirteen-year-old Valkyrie he had nurtured. But he rallied sufficiently to answer her. 'You know your grandmother's not well. She couldn't babysit. And your mother had her duties looking after her. She—'

'Gran's *your* mother. Why couldn't you look after her for a change? It's not as if there's much wrong with her anyway, and she adores the baby, but she's barely seen her since she's been here. I don't think Gran understands any more than I do.'

'That's just it – you *don't* understand. Haven't I told you that your grandmother's nerves are all in a jangle? She's of an age to suffer difficult problems. You know how Leela cried and cried, yet you expected your grandmother to cope with that for hours on end.'

'Oh.' This seemed to bring Kamala up short. 'Are you trying to say that Gran's going through the change?' For a moment, all her youthful certainty faded. But, young as she was, she quickly rallied. 'My friend Annie's gran sailed through it. A course of HRT would set Gran right.'

Her father looked taken aback. 'What do you know of these matters, girl?'

'More than you, probably, Dad,' was Kamala's quick reply.

'Enough of this. How dare you speak to your father like so? You shame us in front of these people. Go to your room.' Kamala's grandfather intervened, his voice harsh, his tone that of someone used to being obeyed.

For a moment a transfixed Kamala looked as if she might defy her forbidding grandfather, but then he broke into rapid Hindi. Whatever he said had the desired effect. For, after flinging one desperate, anguished look at her mother, Kamala fled the room, her tears echoing back at them from the vaulted entrance hall before she slammed into her bedroom and banged the door.

There was an embarrassed silence after her abrupt departure. But within a few moments, Mr Khan senior had broken it. 'I apologise for my granddaughter,' he said to Casey. 'You should send her out to us in India,' he told his son. 'There she would learn how to behave so she does not bring such shame upon us. Remember the family, my son,' he sternly rebuked Rathi Khan. 'How many times must I remind you of its importance?'

Casey thought it was time they left the family to it. After the abrupt departure of the outspoken Kamala, the rest of the family seemed shaken and subdued and unlikely to reveal anything more. They were entitled to some privacy, anyway. After uttering more condolences, Casey told the family they would let themselves out. He nodded to Catt and WPC Singh. They made for the front door and shut it quietly behind them.

Five

They had just reached the car when Dan Khan opened the front door and walked towards them, his small daughter still in his arms. 'Wait, Inspector.'

Casey stood by the car door. He wondered what further revelations he was about to hear. 'Was there something else you wished to tell me, sir?'

Now that he had Casey's uninterrupted attention, Dan Khan didn't seem sure what he wanted to say. After hugging his daughter and smoothing her hair, finally, with what must be unnatural diffidence, he said, 'It was more something I wanted to ask.' He paused, then rushed on as if he had to force the words out. 'I wondered whether there was any possibility that my sister might have killed herself.'

Casey shot a warning glance at Catt, who looked as if he might venture an opinion, before he asked, 'Do you have any reason to think that she might have?'

Dan Khan shrugged his elegantly clad shoulders. 'I don't know. Maybe. You heard my little sister in there. She said Chandra was lonely. She wasn't suited to living alone. She had just lost her husband, and no matter what Kamala said, there was affection between Chandra and Magan. She was depressed about the future. And then, of course, with Leela crying so much she didn't get much rest. All in all a recipe for desperation.'

Casey wondered why, if this was the case, her mother or grandmother hadn't babysat occasionally and given her a break. Why she had been left in such isolation with just a couple of visits from her parents. Apart from being at a difficult time of life, Mrs Khan senior appeared healthy and fit enough to be able to look after one small child, as did Mrs Rathi Khan and Devdan's wife. He waited. He sensed there was more to come. He was right.

Dan Khan, like his sister, had large, lustrous, thickly lashed eyes. They gained a sheen of moisture as he told them, 'My sister was a widow, Inspector. A widow with a baby daughter. I don't expect you to understand what that means in our society, but we're Hindus. It is not usual for Hindu widows to remarry. Maybe it's better she's dead. No one else would want her now. My parents and grandparents like to believe she's in paradise. Perhaps they're right. God knows, as a widow with a small daughter, Chandra was unlikely to find much paradise down here. Think of the dowry my father would have to find, even if he could find a man willing to take them both on. He was trying to persuade my sister into an arranged marriage in India. With a much older man. It would have been much the best solution.'

For Rathi Khan, certainly, if not for Chandra, was Casey's immediate thought.

Dan Khan's soulful gaze rested on his sweet-faced little daughter for a moment, as if seeing for the first time what might be *her* future. His cheek clenched and unclenched as if he didn't much like what he saw. 'My mother was very keen, too. It would have been much cheaper, you see, for her to marry someone in India. Much cheaper than here in England where the dowry is so high. They were worried that if my father didn't arrange something that she might dishonour the family in some way with an unsuitable man.'

Had she? Casey wondered. Was that partly what her mother-in-law's accusations had been about? Had Dan Khan found out about this anonymous, unsuitable man? Had the rest of her family? Her in-laws? He questioned Dan Khan some more.

Bitterly, he denied it.

Casey wasn't sure he believed him. Dan Khan seemed strangely resentful of his sister, even though it was clear he

49

had loved her. Had he been jealous of Chandra? Jealous of her sudden freedom and the opportunity it presented to find herself a lover more to her taste? In spite of her agreeing to an arranged marriage, from her photo and from what he had learned about her, Casey was sure that Chandra Bansi had not been the usual meek and biddable Asian stereotype, so it struck him as possible that she *had* taken a lover.

And if such a lover existed, he could be the real reason Rathi Khan had tried to keep the sisters apart. If Chandra had damaged her reputation by some unwise liaison, he wouldn't want his younger daughter's chances sullied by the connection. And as to what her family might do to Chandra . . .

'And was your sister willing for your father to try to find another husband for her?'

'No,' Devdan admitted. 'But it is possible she would have come round in time. She was aware that otherwise she might face the rest of her life alone.' Tautly, he added, 'Strange she didn't appreciate that there are worse fates than living alone. Of course, it's different for a woman, but if I—' he broke off. But Casey could guess at the rest – *if I had gained my freedom from an unwanted partner, I'd count my blessings.*

Casey could see why Chandra might have been depressed. Poor girl, what a situation to have to face just after losing her husband; even a husband she perhaps hadn't loved. Devdan Khan seemed angry that his sister had gained a freedom he had envied and hadn't appreciated it. But if what her brother said was right and there had been no lover, would her admittedly bleak Hobson's choice of futures have depressed her enough for her to kill herself and take her baby with her? And in such a way?

Then, of course, there was the alternative, that having dishonoured her family, they had helped her and her shame on a speedy journey to the next world.

He studied Devdan Khan thoughtfully for a moment, then said, 'These accusations of Chandra's in-laws – what did they consist of exactly?'

'I told you.'

'Tell me again.'

Briefly, Dan Khan's eyes showed a hunted look. His expression wary, he said, 'Nothing. Really. That she was undutiful, I suppose. Not a traditional Indian wife. Chandra had opinions and expressed them, that is all.'

'They didn't accuse her of taking up with an unsuitable man as your parents feared?' Casey hadn't expected an outright admission. Even so, in the circumstances, Dan Khan revealed more than was wise.

'No. That is . . .' he broke off. 'Chandra was not as demure as her mother-in-law expected. I suppose she could be quite flirtatious, but that was all. If I or my father had thought she was more than that we would naturally remonstrate with her.'

Dan Khan wasn't quite as modern and English in his attitudes as his adopted name and sharp suit indicated. Casey thought that most Asian men, if they caught one of their womenfolk compromising their 'honour', would do rather more than remonstrate.

Was Dan Khan's question as to whether his sister might have killed herself sincere or merely designed to throw them off track? In any case, he had few consoling words to offer him. And after Dan Khan had turned disconsolately away and walked back to the house with his child, he climbed in the car and directed Catt to return to the flat in Ainsley Terrace.

Casey didn't mention the expression he had caught on Rani Khan's face. As, no doubt, Superintendent Brown-Smith would in due course point out, Thomas Catt had a tendency to be woefully politically incorrect in his suspicions. But even if he hadn't imagined it, Casey was aware that it probably indicated nothing more than the spiteful satisfaction of the plain woman when the more beautiful, loved, one is no longer there, no longer taking the love that was rightfully hers.

After Catt had turned the car and headed back to the scene, he remarked, 'A parent's loss of a child is said to be the most painful loss of all. Personally, I've always thought the opposite was true – that a child's loss of his parents is far worse. Particularly if they were the loving sort of parents.'

Surprised, Casey glanced at Catt. He said nothing. It was rare for Catt to mention something so close to the bone. Catt had told him he didn't remember his parents; how could he, when they had abandoned him as a small child? Was he implying that Chandra had somehow lost her parents? Lost their love because of some action of her own? Casey asked him.

Catt nodded. 'Her father said she was wilful and too Westernized. He insisted the younger girl stayed away from her. Maybe, if her in-laws' accusations were more than just their grief talking . . .?'

Casey wondered if Catt had been reading psychology books, but immediately rejected the idea. Catt was not a fan of such things, not since being labelled by a psychologist in his childhood. ThomCatt didn't do labels or overly simplistic conclusions about complex human emotions. He would be the last person to label a girl he had never met.

Thoughtfully, Casey half-turned in his seat to question Shazia Singh. 'Did you catch any of the family's Hindi conversation?'

She nodded. 'The son, Devdan, said much the same as he said in English. The old lady was upset. She wanted to know how Chandra and the baby had died. Her son wouldn't tell her, of course. Maybe he couldn't see that it might have comforted her to know that Chandra had died in such a traditional way, burning in a fire, so soon after her husband's death.'

Casey couldn't imagine how anyone might find comfort in such a death, but he assumed Shazia Singh knew what she was talking about. And now he changed the subject. 'We've heard what Hindu widows can expect. What about Hindu wi-dowers?' he asked her. 'Are they allowed to remarry?'

Pretty, bold-eyed Shazia gave him a smile that had a touch of Catt's cynicism. 'It's a man's world, Inspector, which is something Chandra's brother seems to have forgotten. Naturally they can remarry. But, generally speaking, for a Hindu woman, her husband is her career. Her obligation is to serve her husband and his family and provide him with children, especially sons.'

'Like something out of *The Stepford Wives*,' commented Catt.

'But with much more emotion felt, obviously,' was Shazia's tart rejoinder. 'Many believe the sole joy of the Hindu wife is meant to be to please her husband and to perform whatever services he demands. Even after his death, she is attached to him, bonded to him. A widow is expected to wear white, the colour of death, purity and grief, and to mourn her husband for the rest of her days. She must give up all forms of personal adornment, such as the wearing of jewellery or make-up. She is forbidden to attend social events, even the weddings of her own children.'

'But surely all those taboos wouldn't apply here and now?' Casey questioned. 'We're in the second millennium, after all.'

Shazia shrugged. 'Religious teaching takes little notice of the time or the place, Inspector. Doesn't the Catholic Church still hold medieval views on homosexuality? On sin? On carnality? Sex, not for pleasure, but for the procreation of children?'

'Thank God – or somebody – that I'm with the Church of England,' Catt put in irreverently. 'My lot don't even seem to believe in Him, never mind sin.'

'Anyway, go on,' Casey encouraged Shazia. 'What other experiences await a Hindu widow?'

'In India they are often hounded from their home villages and lose all their possessions. Much of their mistreatment comes down to money and inheritance.'

'Don't most things, in the end?' Catt muttered as a spasm of pain crossed his face.

As well as being irresponsible, Catt's parents had been feckless and poor. Catt had confided one evening after downing too many lagers that they had abandoned him with a badly spelled note pinned to his clothing, saying, 'He costs too much. We can't afford to keep him.'

But maybe ThomCatt had a point. Casey, with all the other aspects, had yet to look at every possible angle. Had Chandra inherited anything? Had her husband anything for her to inherit? It was essential to discover what the situation was, yet to ask her family or in-laws, who were the obvious ones to supply the answer, was unlikely to earn him any awards for diplomacy. Besides, how could he know what they told him was the truth?

It was something else to be checked out. If her late husband hadn't made a will, Chandra would still have inherited a lot under the intestacy laws. The late Magan Bansi's father was a businessman; had his son owned part of that business? Perhaps made over as a marriage gift? He made a mental note to check it out before he asked Shazia Singh to continue.

'Widows are commonly regarded as inauspicious. In fact, to quote an early Hindu text – the *Skanda Purana* – "The widow is more inauspicious than all other inauspicious things." It goes on, "At the sight of a widow, no success can be had in any undertaking, excepting one's mother, all widows are void of auspiciousness. A wise man should avoid even her blessings like the poison of a snake."'

She broke into the shocked silence that greeted this to add, 'To escape the life of outcasts in their villages, many Hindu widows congregate in a place called Vrindavan, a holy city, Krishna's birthplace, in central India, or Varanasi, the "City of Lights"', as Dan Khan mentioned. There, if they are lucky, they might earn a few rupees for hours of chanting a day in one of the many temples.

'The Hindu ban on the remarriage of widows was removed by a British law in the late 1800s, but the taboo on remarriage is still strong. For a widow to remarry frequently brings dishonour on her family. It is believed, and not just by the poor and uneducated, that a woman's husband dies because she has bad karma. And if she has bad karma, what is the point of marrying again? She is likely only to bring the same ill luck to a second husband. It being her fault her first husband died, you see?'

'Even if a man's own stupidity caused his death?' Casey asked.

Shazia nodded. 'She loses all her status and begins a new life – one where she waits for death, fated to mourn the death of her husband till the end of her days. Widows are traditionally regarded as witches and despised by everyone. People still believe that widows are cursed or diseased and that even by simply speaking to them one will be contaminated. You can see why even an older man in India would require a substantial dowry to take on such a wife, even a beautiful one like Chandra Bansi.'

Casey had learned more than he had bargained for. But it seemed that Shazia Singh wasn't finished yet. 'Of course,' she went on, 'it used to be the custom that widows committed sati – immolated themselves on their husband's funeral pyre. A Hindu widow was one of the "living dead", you see, so it was better for all concerned that she should actually *be* dead. Cheaper, too, as far as any inheritance goes. Apart from that, a widow's immolation on her husband's funeral pyre freed his family from the cycle of birth and rebirth. Her sacrifice guaranteed that a woman, her husband and seven generations of the family after would have a direct passport to heaven.' Shazia paused. 'You can see how a woman would find it difficult to resist doing her "duty". But when the British outlawed sati, instead of a quick death and glorification they gave widows a long lingering one and vilification. Many Indian widows don't think it was a fair exchange.' She gave a sad little smile. It held all the tragedy of India. 'It is their karma, you see. Something to be accepted with stoicism. And so they do accept it, praying only for death and an end to their earthbound misery.'

Casey studied her for a moment before he nodded thoughtfully and turned back in his seat. Unaware of the streets they passed, he sat mute. Shazia Singh had certainly provided them with a few motives for murder. She had even made plain that suicide could indeed be a strong possibility.

Was it possible that Chandra *had* chosen the old custom? He frowned and stared unseeingly ahead. Then, before him hovered the remembered image of Chandra's photograph. He took the picture from his pocket and studied it again. And as her bold gaze with its hint of challenge met his, he shook his head. Even lately, sad as her life had become, he felt a quiet certainty that given a choice, the girl in the photograph would choose life – however grim – over death. Hadn't Angela Neerey claimed that Chandra had been trying to plan her future? Besides, the vacuum flask with its petrol dregs which had been discarded in the alley behind her flat didn't point to self-immolation. But neither, given that the husband's funeral pyre would have been the clinical procedure at the local crematorium, did it indicate that she had been persuaded to do her traditional widow's 'duty'.

But even if the flask with its petrol dregs turned out to be no more than coincidence or a particularly cruel joke, Andy Simmonds' comment that there was no logical reason for the fire to start where it had pointed to arson. Confirmation or otherwise of that would have to wait for the forensic team. He hoped they would come up with some firm answers quickly.

Beside him, ThomCatt, ever the cynic, was still keen to push his own suspicions. As he pulled up at the traffic lights, he glanced at Casey and said, 'I still think we ought to check out the father's finances. Discreetly, of course. Maybe they're not as healthy as that expensive house would indicate. You noticed his car's several years old?' Casey nodded. 'Maybe he couldn't afford to find another dowry for Chandra and was merely going through the motions to stop his wife nagging him. Could be he decided the old ways with widows were the best for all concerned – himself, his daughter and the bank balance. And then there's the insurance on the flat. He could have decided to have the place torched to free up some money, believing his daughter and the baby would be out.'

Embarrassed that Catt should be so insensitive in front of

Shazia Singh, Casey asked quietly, 'And did you see anything in the family garage to indicate such a possibility?'

'Not a lot,' Catt admitted as the lights changed and he drove off. 'But there were what appeared to be petrol stains on the floor. And there were some empty cans stacked in the corner.'

'Hardly conclusive. Maybe he had just stockpiled some cans in case there was another petrol shortage. I did the same. It's a messy business decanting petrol into a car's tank without a funnel. My garage floor's stained, too.'

Strangely – for ThomCatt hadn't gained the feline shortening of his given name by lacking a cat's sharpness – he had nothing to say regarding the intriguing comment made by Chandra's sister. What has Chandra done *now*? she had asked. Casey wondered what Chandra could possibly have done *before* to warrant such a question. However, for the moment he didn't invite Catt or Shazia to share in his speculation. Anyway, it seemed likely that her in-laws would be keen to dish any dirt going. Unless, of course, they *did* have something to do with Chandra's death, in which case he supposed he could expect them to backtrack on any accusations they had previously made about their daughter-in-law.

Catt had voiced no further argument by the time they arrived back in Ainsley Terrace. As he got out, Casey told him to drive WPC Singh back to the station and, in a quiet undertone, he agreed that Catt could begin to check out the father's finances and any inheritance that Chandra might have been left by her husband. While he was at it, he could arrange for them to see Chandra's in-laws, the Bansis.

After giving his instructions, Casey headed back to the flat to have another word with the team. He hoped they would have made some progress. He needed some speedy answers on this case or it wouldn't be long before there were others besides Catt raising ugly suspicions on little or no evidence. He was already starting to do so himself.

Six

I t was now nearly seven p.m. Dr Merriman had long since departed, but the forensic boys were still hard at work. When Casey returned to Chandra's flat they had the floorboards up and were carefully packing what they found – charred wood, carpet, paper – that had fallen through the cracks.

'How are you doing?' Casey asked Andy Simmonds. 'Found anything else yet to indicate arson?'

'Not yet. Trouble is, when accelerants like petrol or kerosene evaporate they produce hydrocarbons. And hydrocarbons have a low molecular weight.'

'And that's bad?'

Andy nodded. 'Hydrocarbons are very volatile, you see, which means evidence of accelerant use is hard to find.'

'So you have no conclusive proof that this was arson?'

Simmonds shook his head. 'Not yet, anyway.'

'So what now? Is there any hope that you'll find something?'

'There's always hope, Inspector.' Andy nodded towards the raised floorboards and told him, 'It just means we have to try harder. That's why we're looking under floorboards and rugs, in corners and so on, in the hope that not all the accelerant has evaporated and that at least some of the liquid hasn't burned off. With luck, it may have soaked into surfaces which can then be treated in the lab.' He hefted one of the containers he had been using. 'Here's where we'll find any evidence of the use of an accelerant, like petrol. These little beauties prevent vaporization, so we can get fibres back to the lab for testing. Then we get the gas chromatograph to work on them and it'll separate out the individual traces on these fibres. All we need is an infinitesimal amount of accelerant and we'll have confirmation that this was arson. Then we might nail whoever did this.'

Casey could only hope he was right. It was late, but the day still held another duty before he could go home. Superintendent Brown-Smith had contacted Casey on his mobile as soon as news of the fire had filtered through to him. He was waiting now, for Casey's return and his report.

And as he knocked and entered Brown-Smith's office, Casey braced himself.

Casey had been too busy all day to see a newspaper, so when Superintendent Brown-Smith thumped a copy of the local evening rag on his desk, Casey was shocked to see the headline SATI IN SUBURBIA? glare out at him from the front page.

He sighed quietly. Their local newspaper was owned and edited by Gwyn Owen, an independently wealthy hothead who was, if possible, even less politically correct than Thomas Catt. With such a headline on the first day of the case he knew the super's usual mixed metaphors when upset were likely to form a particularly rich soup.

'I'll have him for this,' the super threatened. 'The man's a troublemaker of the last orders. I've already spoken to Anthony Lorn about it.'

Tony Lorn was their local Labour MP, one of the super's many PC acquaintances. Casey thought it unlikely that even a red-hot PC barrister like Lorn would find a charge in the statute book that would hold water. He doubted Superintendent Brown-Smith believed it and was just venting his spleen. Besides, the editor was merely putting forward a possibility – one which Casey was also considering.

Still, it was unfortunate timing. Obviously the case would be picked up in the next day's nationals, but Casey was confident that Superintendent Brown-Smith would have made sure they wouldn't repeat the local editor's speculation. Casey would have talked to the editor, tried to reason with him so that he refrained from further conjecture along similar lines, but from the thunderous expression opposite, he suspected such an intervention would not only be pointless but come too late, as Brown-Smith's next words confirmed.

'Do you know what Owen had the cheek to tell me when I spoke to him?'

Casey shook his head.

'That *I* was the racist – only I was racially prejudiced against my *own* people. Can you believe it?'

Wisely, Casey kept silent. Not that the super really expected an answer, certainly not one that agreed with the editor's opinion. But it was a view ThomCatt certainly shared and had frequently expressed. There was more than an element of truth in it, too. Unfortunately, ThomCatt had a way of speaking his mind without thought for who might be listening. He would have to speak to him about it – and about his attitude – before someone else did.

'After seeing that . . . that rag,' the super didn't trouble to name the offending local organ as he went on, 'you'll understand me when I say I want you to tread very warily on this investigation. The last thing we want is a repeat of the Stephen Lawrence fiasco and its subsequent media witch-hunt. I want the media to have not one single aspect of this case to criticize. Tread softly when speaking to the ethnic community. Kid gloves are what's needed here. Do I make myself clear?'

Casey nodded. Aware that with the super in this mood it was pointless to try to reason with him, he let much of the predictable politically correct platitudes wash over him. But, as he took in this latest mixed metaphor and briefly wondered whether the superintendent expected him to be shod in kid gloves during any conversation about the deaths with one of the ethnic community, other more pressing questions occurred to him. They would earn him no brownie points, but he voiced them anyway. 'And what if, during the course of this investigation, it becomes clear that a member of the ethnic community – even a member of the victims' own family – killed them?' The tiniest tinge of irony infected Casey's voice as he added, 'I presume charging them will be permitted?'

Superintendent Brown-Smith shot him a venomous look. Casey swallowed a sigh, aware he had spoken the unspeakable. It was clear the prospect of meting out justice in such an eventuality appalled the superintendent. Determinedly on the way up the career ladder these murders really were the case from hell for him. As the super's wall clock – a much-cherished family heirloom – loudly ticked away the seconds, Casey became convinced that, should such an unwelcome conclusion become unavoidable, he was about to be urged to stage a discreet cover-up.

But even Superintendent Brown-Smith, in full pursuit of the politically correct and expedient, wouldn't be that foolhardy. Although he got himself under control, his voice was harsh from the realization that here was his own annus horribilis. 'Obviously, if you reach such a point that no other conclusion is possible I shall require you to confer with me first, before you make any arrests. I want no precipitate action. In fact, I shall want you to give me a full briefing at the end of each day. Less than one hundred per cent certainty of guilt in this case is not an option.'

Casey couldn't help but wonder if the superintendent would apply the same demanding criteria should white arsonists turn out to be the culprits. A tic started up at the corner of the superintendent's left eye as he added, 'Jobs could be on the line here, Casey.'

Casey's stomach essayed a tortured, spasmodic accompaniment to Superintendent Brown-Smith's tic, as if in acknowledgement that Casey was being lined up to be the fall guy if – when – such a convenience should be required.

'Obviously, you'll need a team high on diplomacy and understanding of racial sensitivities – you *have* been on a recent racial awareness course, haven't you Casey?'

'Last month, sir.'

'Mm.' The superintendent frowned. 'You usually work with Sergeant Catt, do you not?'

Casey nodded. He suspected he could guess what was coming. Thomas Catt had been on two racial awareness courses. Casey had reason to suspect that had only been because ThomCatt had not shown a sufficient grasp of the importance of ethnic sensitivities the first time round, something which the superintendent seemed only too aware of as he went on. 'I think, in the circumstances, owing to the various delicate aspects inherent in this investigation, I would prefer that Sergeant Catt worked on something else. Catt can be a little tactless, can he not?'

Casey, already required to conduct the investigation with both – gloved – hands tied behind his back, dug his heels in at this. He was damned if he was going to be deprived of his right-hand man along with everything else. Thomas Catt might be a sad loss to the *corps diplomatique* and his PC sensitivities might still be a bit suspect, but he was a first-rate policeman. Besides, Casey was used to him. The last thing he needed was to have one of the super's pet blue-eyed fast-track boys foisted on him, dogging his heels and reporting his every utterance back. This case was going to be difficult enough. It would be intolerable with a spy in the camp and no confidant with whom he could speak freely.

But Casey didn't interrupt as the superintendent expanded on the PC theme. For good measure, further mixed metaphors vilified Gwyn Owen, the local editor. Casey hoped his outpouring would get rid of some of his temper and make him more reasonable.

According to Superintendent Brown-Smith, Thomas Catt not only possessed a woeful lack of political correctness, he was too independently minded, too much his own person – a lamentable thing to be in the modern police service. In many ways, so was Casey, only he had taken care to keep his feelings to himself.

Like Casey, Thomas Catt believed in justice – equal justice
– for all. Their mutual, increasingly unfashionable and un-
compromising honesty had bonded them into a solid team.
With his children's home background, Catt had a tendency to
suspect everyone and trust no one, least of all the PC thought
police. Like Casey, he wondered what was the point of trying
to force others to a particular view. People had to come to
realization and understanding in their own time. The PC
lobby didn't seem to grasp that views openly expressed could
be argued with, reasoned with and, ultimately, made for a far
healthier society. Telling Johnny – or Mohammed – he was
barbaric, or racist, or a woman-hater didn't make him less so,
all it was likely to do was add a simmering resentment to the
brew.

Casey was not surprised to discover that Catt found it hard
to trust even him. He wasn't great at trusting others himself.
He probably even shared some of Catt's maverick qualities,
though he believed he concealed them rather better. Casey's
youth had taught him many things, not least the necessity of
developing his own survival techniques. Much like ThomCatt
when he left the children's home at the tender age of sixteen,
he had been forced to learn self-sufficiency, self-reliance and
responsibility. He had often found these hard-won qualities
useful in dealing with Superintendent Brown-Smith.

Their early experiences no doubt made both him and Catt
less willing to swallow whole and unquestioned the politically
correct cant that had flooded the police service in recent years.
And now, as he sensed the super running out of both steam
and the energy required to produce it, he firmly set out his
requirements. 'If I'm to continue to lead this case,' he stressed
the *if*, as if he was going to be allowed to give it up, 'I insist on
working with Catt. We work well together.' Before the superintendent could voice a refusal, Casey added, 'I'll make sure
he keeps in the background when I'm interviewing any of the
Asian community. I'll get him to take a vow of silence if
necessary.' Casey didn't give Brown-Smith the opportunity to

express his scepticism at this, but added what he believed the superintendent was waiting to hear. 'I'll also take full responsibility for him.'

Brown-Smith sat back, gave Casey a narrow-eyed stare before he nodded. 'Very well. Catt's yours. You can also have WPC Singh for the duration of the case. You'll need her language skills.' The unspoken message that Casey had just put his head on a platter hung in the air between them. And as Superintendent Brown-Smith resumed his politically correct exhortations, Casey had ample time for reflection. Disillusionment with the job had steadily increased in recent years, and Casey was no exception. He had started seriously to count his savings and to wonder if he would be able to live on them while he found a less stressful job. Unfortunately, whether his arithmetic was off or his figures didn't compute, his parents' successive inroads into his savings meant he still had fifteen years remaining on the mortgage he had hoped to pay off early.

Casey's thoughts turned to the still-monologizing Brown-Smith – he'd heard it all before so the occasional nod was all that was required – and he reflected on how much the superintendent's office mirrored the man. Like Brown-Smith himself, the office contained pairings of ordinary things joined together to make them look more important. Brown-Smith had pictures of himself in gown and mortar board accepting his degree, closely abutting pictures of him and his wife at a palace garden party in happy juxtaposition with the Queen. This picture-pairing, directly behind the desk so you couldn't fail to see it, had an entire wall to itself.

The wall to Casey's right held several, lesser pictures – of Brown-Smith handing out rosettes at his eldest daughter's pony club gymkhana, alongside one of him shaking the hand of a beaming Asian mayor.

On the occasions he had occupied the super's visitor's chair, Casey had found ample time during the monologues to ponder why not one of the graduation pictures featured a mother or father, when it was known that Brown-Smith had parents and hadn't sprung to life under a gooseberry bush in the garden of some liberal Church of England vicar as Thomas Catt would have it. Strangely, the super's parents weren't apparent in any of the other pictures either. Was it possible that, like himself, the superintendent suffered from unsuitable parents syndrome? It would certainly put another slant on the reason for his late adoption of the double-barrels, an adoption revealed by a close study of the framed graduation certificate with its single-barrelled name. Maybe Brownjob – as Catt irreverently called their superior – had good reason to keep his parents decently buried.

And although he didn't encourage ThomCatt to ridicule their superior, with his own parents weighing heavily on his mind it occurred to Casey that he might just have found the reason why Brown-Smith was so keen to be one of them he was prepared to bow the knee to whatever politically correct dogma the establishment cared to spout. If the super's name change was not merely for show but done for wholly sensible reasons, they might have more in common than he had previously believed. The thought almost made him warm to the man.

Superintendent Brown-Smith's PC monologue finally came to an end. Casey dragged his gaze from the contemplation of the glassy, dust-free picture gallery just as the super uttered his name and was at last allowed to escape.

The first day of the case had been long and tiring. And when Casey finally arrived home, feeling bushed and frustrated by too many questions with – as yet – no answers and the pressures already beginning to build, he saw as he approached his front door that the day's frustrations had scarcely begun. For, squatting on his doorstep, surrounded by assorted baggage, were his parents.

Seven

Casey wondered uneasily whether merely thinking about his parents had somehow spirited them here. His parents, unreconstructed old hippies who still refused to leave the sixties behind despite both being well into middle age, lived on a ramshackle communal smallholding where they had a subsistence, *Good Life* existence. Every so often the community suffered a financial crisis and the inhabitants moved out to stay with various hippie friends. Inevitably, as they had aged, their collection of hippie friends and acquaintances with spare rooms had decreased and Casey had been called upon to pick up the slack. He had bailed his parents out financially a number of times. It saved him from having them as permanent lodgers.

'Why didn't you ring?' And warn me, he added silently to himself as he opened the front door to let them in.

'No bread, man,' his father laconically explained, being too idle to waste words.

He didn't need to add that Casey had, in any case, forbidden them to try making reverse charge calls to the station. All he needed was for it to get out that DCI Casey had a pair of degenerate, drug-taking old hippies for parents . . .

'Hey, my uptight man, don't you have a hug for your mama?'

Casey turned. His mother still looked the same; still wore her kinky, now greying hair long and mostly plaited, which only increased its kinkiness. Today she wore an ankle-length Indian cheesecloth skirt instead of the sari or salwar kameez she mostly favoured since her Indian trips. Under the skirt peeked a pair of vermillion embroidered *jootis*.

Casey smiled sheepishly. 'Hi Mum. It's good to see you.' The swift hug pressed her numerous beads painfully against his shirt-clad chest and he winced.

His mother held him away from her and gazed at him, a suspicious twinkle in the green eyes that Casey had inherited. For all his mother's hippie ideology, she was, unlike his father, sharp enough to appreciate that her son found his parents an embarrassment. His father, on the other hand, even if he were aware of his son's feelings, would probably just shake his head, light another spliff and say, 'Don't get heavy, man. Loosen up.'

Casey's father preferred the world and its problems, including those of his son, to waft past him on a drug-scented breeze. Casey put aside his anxieties, shook his father's hand and clapped him on the shoulder. A mistake, as an odd smell drifted in Casey's direction. He knew his father wasn't much into washing and had got out of the habit of taking regular baths or showers since the last time their water supply had been cut off. Anyway, he always insisted he preferred the purity of rainwater. Only he didn't make much use of their stored rainwater either, because 'heating it up's such a drag, man'.

Casey wrinkled his nose and sniffed, but even this smell was rather ripe for it to emanate from his father's body. It took no more than a second to trace the smell to his father's shaggy Afghan coat. This sixties relic, obviously a recent second-hand purchase, was nonetheless worn with pride, despite the fact it smelled as if the dead animal it came from still inhabited the skin.

His mother gave him a slow wink from kohl-encircled eyes. 'Don't worry, Willow Tree, honey, we won't be cramping your style for long.'

Casey brightened. It was not that he wasn't glad to see them both, not really. They were his parents, after all. It was just that for a policeman – and a senior policeman at that – they were the wrong sort of parents. Much as he suspected Superintendent Brown-Smith's were. And for ageing hippies, whose youth had resounded to chants against the 'pigs', *he* was the wrong sort of son.

He ushered them inside, with a suggestion that they make themselves at home. But not too at home, he silently prayed, as he began to heave their luggage into his hallway.

Carboard boxes.

He had rebelled, by conforming. After an early acceptance of their opt-out and irresponsible lifestyle, he had, in his late teens, rejected it. He had been a source of parental disappointment ever since. As for his parents, they still felt the stigma of having a policeman for a son. It had been the 'pigs' who had harassed them at Woodstock and the Isle of Wight and countless other festivals in their youth. For Casey, it created a guilt trip. And while his brain knew that the guilt he felt in being a disappointment – even a shameful disappointment when his parents had to confess to their equally old, hippie friends that their only son was a pig – was ridiculous. But he felt guilty nonetheless.

Baskets.

Was that how Chandra had felt? he wondered. Her life, too, had made differing demands. Her family and her in-laws required her to conform to their traditional beliefs, while her experiences of growing up a young girl in England raised entirely different expectations. Like him, she must have been continually pushed and pulled in two opposing directions. For Chandra, death had brought the push/pull to an end. And if he wasn't the son his parents would have wanted, Chandra, too, hadn't turned out to be the daughter her parents – or her in-laws – had wanted. She had too many opinions by all accounts, was too spirited and westernized and had only agreed to her arranged marriage when she was at a low ebb, having done badly in her exams. The idea that she was not particularly bright had been brought home to her – deliberately? – by her parents.

Assorted rucksacks.

Her marriage, he suspected, had been unhappy. Her mother-in-law critical. He found it difficult to believe that in her situation she would have welcomed an early pregnancy. Casey wondered whether the pregnancy had been an unhappy accident. Certainly, it must have made her feel even more trapped. And then her husband had died. How had that made her feel? Guilty and responsible, as her in-laws had told her she was? Or gloriously, unexpectedly free from the ties of a marriage she had never actually wanted? But her release from the bonds of marriage, rather than freeing her, had only brought even more pressure.

Was that why her brother had put forward the possibility that Chandra might have killed herself and her baby? Or did the suggestion spring from a desire to turn their suspicions from other possibilities?

God – they'd even brought their record collection.

They must have crept out before the bailiffs arrived and cadged a lift from another of the departing commune. Casey just hoped they didn't stink the place out with dope like last time.

When he had finally heaved all his parents' possessions into the hall and shut the door, Willow Tree Casey went in search of his mother. He found her in his kitchen poking about in his store cupboard.

'Hon. What kind of junk have you got in your larder?' his mother asked in her pseudo-Californian accent as she surveyed the ranks of tinned everything. 'It's all kinda unhealthy.'

Casey restrained the impulse to point out the irony of his druggie mother commenting on the unhealthy junk he chose to put in his body. Instead, quietly, and without fuss, he found some brown macrobiotic rice that Rachel, his musician girl-friend who was fortunately away on tour, had bought last time she was home, set it to boil while he grated cheese and carrot, sliced raw mushrooms and prepared a green salad.

With Rachel away so much with the orchestra, he had got in the habit of looking after himself – anyway, he had been used to doing so from childhood – and several evenings a week he stopped at the small supermarket on the corner of his street. Luckily, given the arrival of his unexpected visitors, he had shopped the previous evening.

After getting his parents settled, and the meal prepared and eaten, Casey slumped tiredly in an armchair before he asked, 'So what happened this time? Did your crops fail again?'

As Casey had good reason to believe that the only crops they grew on their Fenland smallholding with any enthusiasm or success was cannabis, he thought this unlikely. But he couldn't quite bring himself to come the heavy-handed son and ask outright if the bailiffs *had* turned up again demanding payment of debts.

However, his father wasn't so reticent. As he sat on the floor, sorting through their ancient record collection, with the wall light gleaming off the expanding bald spot visible beneath his otherwise long, luxuriant and still black hair, he slowly drawled, 'The crops are fine. Likely to be a good harvest. No, what happened was . . .' And he launched into a long, rambling explanation which Casey lost track of – and interest in – before it was half told. The drugs his father had taken over the years hadn't improved his ability to string a coherent sentence together, much less several. Anyway, he had got the gist of it. He had been right. The bailiffs *had* paid another visit. He wondered how much it would cost him this time to set things right, and winced on discovering the answer.

Casey's mobile phone rang just then. It was Rachel.

'Hi, Will. I heard about the murder case and wasn't sure whether you'd be home yet. Can you talk or are you about to see BB?'

BB was Brian Brownjob, aka Superintendent Brown-Smith. Casey, with Joan Baez singing loudly in one ear and his father's tuneless voice accompanying her in the other, was debating his answer when she asked, 'What's all that noise? Don't tell me you're throwing a party?'

'No,' he replied. It only seemed like it. He stood up and went into the hall, shutting the door behind him. 'It's just the radio.'

'Good. Don't want you learning to enjoy yourself in my absence. Can't chat long. Mr Baton Man's ordered an extra rehearsal. So how's it going? Trust you to draw the short straw. I suppose Brownjob's being bloody?'

'Heading that way. It's good to hear a sane, friendly voice. I miss you.'

'Me too. Listen, I'll have to go.' A furious, hectoring voice was clearly audible down the phone line. Casey guessed it was Mr Baton Man himself. 'I just rang to let you know the tour's being extended. Seems the Brighton and Southampton venues want us after all.'

Casey didn't know whether to be pleased or sorry. He missed Rachel like hell, but it meant he had more time to get his parents out of his hair.

'You needn't sound so disappointed,' she said when he made no comment.

'Sorry, sweetheart. Of course I am. It's just that I'm not likely to be home much myself. I've got a lot on my plate right now.'

'You and me both, kiddo. All right! I'm coming!' This, Casey presumed, was not directed at him but at the orchestral conductor, whose prissy high-pitched tones could be heard even more plainly as he asked sarcastically if Rachel could possibly tear herself away from her latest lover and come and do the job she was paid to do.

'God. He's such a bitchy old queen,' Rachel complained sotto voce. 'Take no notice of that bit about my lovers. You're the only one I want or need.'

'Glad to hear it.'

'I'll ring you later in the week. Bye now.'

'By—' The phone cut off.

Half an hour later, after listening to yet more of his parents' scratchy records, Casey pleaded tiredness at the end of a long day and retired to bed. But not to sleep. He could hear another old Joan Baez record playing none too softly downstairs, followed by The Mamas and the Papas' hit 'California Dreamin''. The volume rose as the hours passed. Casey sighed, aware he would have to remind his parents of the house rules in the morning.

He only hoped they weren't still here when Rachel returned from her tour. Rachel was a particular girl, who liked everything spick and span. His semi-detached was too small to contain them all in harmony.

Was Chandra's mother-in-law's house small, too? he wondered. In cramped surroundings people couldn't get away from one another. Proximity, he recognized as the music thumped from downstairs, brought irritations, resentments. Anger festers and grows. Was that what had happened in Chandra's case? Had her grief-crazed in-laws decided to consign Chandra to the flames so that, in death, she could perform her wifely duties as she had failed to do in life?

With the music thumping its accompaniment to his thoughts, his mind turned to India and the things he had witnessed there as a child. Although he had found much of the culture and most of the people full of charm, there was one aspect of the Hindu creed that still appalled him. The one that said that if you were old, sick, poor, hungry, it was your own fault; your way of living your previous life or lives had earned you a punishing karma in this one.

Casey had always found that 'it's your own fault you're a cripple' aspect of Hinduism very hard to take. It was one reason why he had never returned to India, even though there were many aspects of the country he *had* liked. He had met with great kindness and generosity, often from people who had little enough, but who were perfectly willing to share that little with you. It was the sort of place that knocked your socks off – and then offered to wash them for you.

The way that innocent sections of society were treated, shunned even, was something he found unacceptable. Yet, he acknowledged as he turned over again and tried to get comfortable, theirs wasn't the only culture guilty of prejudice. In India it was widows and the untouchables. In England, certainly before they became 'fashionable', the section that society treated as pariahs had been homosexuals. Like widows, they too – and not so long ago – had been shunned by society, their employers, even their families. It was simply a case of different cultures, different mores.

Casey's father had sailed blithely through all the experiences India had thrown at them, much as he sailed through everything else. But Casey suspected that his mother, too, had been deeply affected by her time in the country.

She had started a charity while she was there, begging and borrowing from wealthy tourists in order to feed some of the street children. Her intentions had been good, but the administration of anything had never been her strong point. Casey put it down to all the drugs she had experimented with in her youth. Having parents who were out of their heads for most of the time had concentrated Casey's wonderfully. And apart from being more or less force-fed weed in his teens, he had turned away from drugs entirely. After being brought up by parents who did everything to excess on a daily basis, he had a secret fear that this trait might be inherited.

Too tired to think any more, he turned over once more and thrust a pillow over his ears. He must get some sleep. But, feeling obliged to keep his nose flared to catch the familiar scent of cannabis, Casey passed a restless night.

The morning wasn't a towering success either. His mother had risen early. She tried to do her earth mother bit and get him breakfast, but his complicated modern cooker had defeated her. All he got was burnt scrambled eggs and stewed black tea. She had dropped the milk bottle while trying to rescue his eggs and the floor lay under a slippery ocean of white.

Casey told her not to worry, that he'd get something at the station, and fled. As he drove off he realized that in the confusion he had forgotten to remind her of the house rules. He hadn't even found out what their plans were, he realized. This brought a taut smile. What plans? His parents had always believed in going with the flow. They never planned, never worried. What for? they had always asked the earnest, youthful Casey. Worrying changed nothing. All it did was give you wrinkles and constipation. Stay cool, he had been advised. Have a drag.

Maybe he should try these lines on the superintendent when he demanded news of the case's progress. Casey tried to imagine Brown-Smith's face if he did so, especially when he passed the weed . . .

With his parents' arrival, Casey found himself empathizing more and more with Chandra Bansi. She had been caught between two worlds. He wondered what resolution about her life she would have come to if she had lived. But she no longer had a life *to* resolve. With death, all her problems had become his. His the resolution, too.

In a small act of rebellion, Casey shrugged off his defensively adopted conservatism and tuned from Radio 4 to a station playing defiant heavy metal for the rest of the journey. At least it took his mind off the grim events awaiting him later in the morning when the two post-mortems were scheduled.

Just as they passed reception on the way to the car park and the scheduled post-mortems, they heard raised voices. And when Casey heard a young male voice mention Chandra's name, he held out a hand to stop Catt in his tracks, pressed his ear to the crack in the door and eavesdropped shamelessly. Curious, Casey lifted his head and stared through the glass panel, easing the door open a little as he did so.

The young man – he could only have been in his early twenties – swept a trembling hand through a thick mane of fair hair. From the way it stood up on end, this was not the first such sweeping. 'I've got to know what happened,' he repeated. 'Surely the report in the paper must be wrong? Chandra can't be dead? My God, surely she can't be dead?' His fists clenched and he banged one on the desk. 'Tell me. You've got to tell me what happened.'

The desk sergeant, Sergeant Allen, a patient, kindly, middle-aged man, tried to calm him down. 'If you'll just take a few deep breaths and start again, sir, I might be able to help you. Now, first things first – who are you? And what is your connection with the young lady?' The desk sergeant peered expectantly at his interrogator over his half-moon spectacles and waited.

After a brief struggle, the young man capitulated. 'My name's Mark Farrell. I'm a friend of Chandra's. Mrs Chandra Bansi,' he enlarged. 'The girl the papers say died in a fire at her flat. I've known her since we were at infant school.' Tears filled his eyes and fell in fat globules down his cheeks. He paused, took a deep steadying breath and went on more calmly. 'I've been abroad on business and have just got back. First I heard of it was when I finally got the chance to pick up a newspaper. I want to know exactly what happened.'

After patting the young man's arm, the sergeant reached under the desk and found a box of tissues. He handed over a couple, told him, 'DCI Casey is dealing with this matter. I believe he'll want to speak to you.' As he picked up the phone, he added, 'Take a seat and I'll see if he's available.'

Casey pushed open the door to reception and walked into the desk sergeant's line of view as if he and Catt had just come down the stairs and heard the last few words. 'No need for that Sergeant Allen. Here I am.'

Five minutes later, Mark Farrell was sitting in the visitor's chair in Casey's office. Catt was seated at his corner desk, ready to take notes. Farrell had a cup of tea from the canteen in front of him and had calmed down considerably.

Casey glanced at his watch. They were due to attend the

post-mortems in half an hour. Casey, who prided himself on his timekeeping, judged they still had plenty of time and could afford to hear what Farrell had to say. Besides, as he had known the dead girl his information could be important.

'I'm glad you came in, Mr Farrell,' Casey told him. 'I was intending to contact Chandra's friends. I'd be interested to learn all that you can tell me about Mrs Bansi. It's often the case that the more you know about a victim the greater your chance of catching whoever's responsible for their death.' He paused. 'What was she like? What was her state of mind before her death?'

Farrell blinked as Casey addressed him. He had been sunk into himself and took a moment to recollect where he was and why. When he remembered, his face seemed to fall in on itself as fresh grief engulfed him.

Casey sat quietly till it passed, then he repeated his questions.

'She was very nervy,' Farrell told him. 'It wasn't like her.' His tissues now a useless soggy mess, he wiped his nose with the back of his hand and sniffed hard. 'Chandra was always pretty outgoing and confident, even after her marriage.'

'Did she mention what the problem was? Why she was nervy?'

Farrell shook his head. 'Not really. We were close, but she just clammed up. I don't think she liked living on her own with the baby. It's a bit of a rough neighbourhood. You'd think her father would have more sense than to stick her there. But then she wasn't keen on returning to her parents' place, either. I got the impression she was getting a lot of pressure from her family. She told me they wanted her to marry again.' Farrell's good looks were marred by a scowl. 'You'd think one unhappy arranged marriage would be enough for them.'

'Was it so unhappy?' Casey questioned, keen to get confirmation of this from another source.

'That's the impression I got. Her husband was the jealous kind. Very possessive. Always checking up on her. Chandra found it irksome. She'd been used to a lot more freedom. Her husband certainly didn't like her being friendly with me.' He pulled a face. 'Neither did her parents. Gave her a lot of grief over it.' He scowled again. 'Between the lot of them I hardly saw her any more. And then they were pushing her to marry some old bloke in India. If they managed to persuade her I knew I'd never see her again and I valued our friendship too much for that to happen.'

How friendly *had* they been? Casey wondered. Like most police officers working in multi-ethnic communities, he was only too aware of the violence interracial relationships could cause. Plenty of Asian girls had had bounty hunters set on them when they ran away after refusing to agree to arranged marriages. Others had been murdered by their families.

Murdered by their families, he repeated to himself. Was this case going to turn out to be yet another domestic tragedy? A case of a thoroughly westernized young woman expected to live up to old-fashioned, increasingly alien ideals, and failing? Such marriages were an increasing source of contention in Asian families. He didn't see any easy solution to it until the younger, westernized generation were raising teenagers themselves.

Casey's thoughts returned to the young man sitting in front of him. 'So how friendly were you with Chandra, Mr Farrell? You say her family didn't approve of her remaining friends with you?'

Mark Farrell nodded. 'Chandra told me she got a lot of stick from them and from her in-laws. I did my best to cool it. But it was difficult. Hell, I fancied her like mad. I always have. She was a beautiful girl.' He shrugged. 'OK, I admit I wanted more than friendship. I thought maybe . . .' Abruptly, he broke off. When he spoke again, Farrell sounded even more sullen. 'She could be a bit of a tease. She sometimes led me on, let me kiss her and then she'd pull the plug.'

It was clear that Farrell had resented Chandra's treatment of him. He had openly admitted he had wanted more. As he said, Chandra had been a beautiful girl, outgoing, vivacious. And Mark Farrell was a good-looking young man, even with eyes red-rimmed from weeping, a young man likely to be used to getting any girl he wanted.

Could he be the unsuitable man her family had feared might entice Chandra from the path of duty? Had he pushed his suit after Chandra's husband had died and she was in the flat alone but for her baby? Had she rejected him? Or had she, worn down on all fronts, finally capitulated and then, with time to regret her capitulation, had she rejected him again? After tasting that which he had lusted after for so long it was unlikely the handsome, rather petulant Farrell would take such a rejection lightly.

Casey stared speculatively at Farrell. Because it wasn't only women scorned who reacted with rage. The media coverage of rejected male suitors who turned into obsessive stalkers was lengthy and depressing. Was it possible Mark Farrell was one such?

Casey resolved to have another word with Angela Neerey, Chandra's neighbour. If anyone was able to enlighten them further as to Mark Farrell's position in Chandra's life, she was the one.

But before they did that, they had another pressing engagement.

These post-mortems were going to be rough, Casey knew. The victims' bodies had looked bad enough in the flat. Here, under the harsh lights, there would be no aspect of the charred flesh left to a more kindly imagination.

Casey and Catt stood silently as the mortuary assistant expertly positioned the body of the adult fire victim for the photographs before Dr Merriman began his preliminary examination. It would already have been weighed and X-rayed. Then, he made the classic Y-shaped incision across the breast from shoulder to shoulder and down the abdomen to the pubis. The saw buzzed through the ribs and cartilage, exposing the internal organs; the part that always made Casey feel like a particularly grisly voyeur.

Dr Merriman bent over the body and began to murmur a few asides for his report. 'Healthy,' he noted, as he let his gaze rest briefly on the most unhealthy-looking remains Casey had ever seen. 'No signs of disease.'

One by one the organs were removed, various samples taken. Dr Merriman rotated the pelvis, where the flesh had burned away, and he did a quick measurement, lowering his head to speak into his chest microphone. 'The diameter of the femoral head is small, indicating that the body is that of a female. The long bones have a small diameter, muscle attachments smooth; also indicative of a female.' He cleared some of the charred flesh and examined the pelvis again. 'Pubic bones wide . . . gently recurved.' He murmured a few words to the mortuary assistant and, briefly, the saw buzzed again. 'Scarring . . . victim has given birth.'

Time wore on. After what seemed an age, the pathologist turned his attention to the victim's skull. Casey winced as the buzz of the saw cut into the top of Chandra's once beautiful head. He blinked, and what remained of her face disappeared like a conjuring trick as the skin and stubble of hair were peeled down over the face, exposing the brain. Casey swallowed and gazed away as he heard the attendant scoop the brain out and on to the table.

'Molar roots completed . . . Bone has honeycombing and no indications of recent fusion of the growth cap. Adult. Sharp orbital borders, small brow ridges, bone smooth. Female.' Merriman shone a torch into the ear. 'Asian . . . epidural haemorrhage . . . no sign of bruising . . . typical indications of carbon monoxide poisoning in the blood and the unburned areas of skin . . .'

Casey's ears pricked up at this. 'It was a combination of the fire and fumes that killed her then? She wasn't killed by a blow to the head?'

Arthur Merriman raised his head. He eased his back and

switched off his microphone as he stood back from the table. 'No.' He closed his eyes briefly, as though to gather his thoughts, then explained, 'Fire has an immensely destructive power, Inspector.' He gestured down at the body. 'As I explained to you at the scene, it tightens and tears the skin like a knife wound. The brain has a large amount of water which boils and expands when exposed to fire and sets up hydrostatic pressure inside the head, which causes the cranial vault to crack. With enough heat, it may even explode.'

There was a stunned silence at this. But Casey had already had this gruesome possibility explained to him once so he collected himself more quickly than Shazia Singh and asked, 'And that's what happened here? The cracking, I mean, not . . .'

Dr Merriman nodded. 'The damage to the skull was caused by an epidural haemorrhage, just under the skin, rather than a subdural haemorrhage. It was caused *after* death and by the fire itself. I've taken blood samples to test for the presence of carbon monoxide, but you can take it from me that the fumes and the fire between them killed her, rather than an assailant with a blunt instrument.' He asked his assistant to turn the body on to its front and he pointed to the small area of unscarred skin on the back. It was a bright, cherry pink. 'As I believe I have explained to you before, the colour is typical of carbon monoxide poisoning. There are also particles of what looks like carbon – soot – in the air passages and lungs. I'll have those tested as well. The victim was female, not a teenager, but not old. Early twenties would be my estimate. She was Asian and certainly borne one child. As to her identity, I've had a dental X-ray taken and sent to the forensic orthodontist. When he compares it to the dental X-ray of the presumed victim, we will hopefully get a match and a confirmed ID.'

Casey looked at the emptied shell of the body, at the hollow head and inside out scalp. The opened out thing on the table *had* no identity. How to reconcile this with the laughing-eyed and beautiful young woman in the photograph? The comparison jarred his senses and built up an anger, a determination to catch whoever was responsible for such an ugly metamorphosis.

But the post-mortem ordeal wasn't over yet. As the table bearing Chandra Bansi's remains was wheeled away and replaced with another, Casey steeled himself for the next post-mortem, that of the baby. Beautiful, bawling Leela, Chandra's infant daughter.

It was over. Thankfully, Casey let himself out into the afternoon air, cool now after the warmth earlier in the day. He breathed deeply, wanting to rid his lungs, his clothes, his mind of the stench of death and its clinical dismemberment. Merriman's conclusions on the cause of the baby's death had been the same as for her mother. He could only hope the fumes had killed them both quickly. The image conjured up when he thought of the baby, those small limbs contorting as the baby burned, was more than he could stomach.

His mobile rang and he reached in his jacket and flipped it open. 'Casey . . . You have? Where are they? . . . Good work. We're on our way in.'

Relief washed over him as he returned the mobile to his jacket pocket. He hadn't realized how high this investigation had stoked the tension. The relief left him feeling extraordinarily tired, but the thought of conducting the interviews with the two youths responsible sent the adrenalin surging through his system and quickly re-energized him.

He told Catt and Shazia, who had followed him out, 'The casualty department of the local hospital turned up trumps. Although they haven't treated any burns victims today, they've at last come up with the information we asked for. Their records show two young white males received treatment for burns just after the first two cases of arson. Must be getting better at their fire-raising, as they didn't pay another visit to casualty after this latest fire.'

'Practise makes perfect,' Catt commented.

As an image of the two bodies in the mortuary flashed before him, Casey said, 'Come on. After what we've just witnessed I'm keen to take a look at the two johnnies responsible. Can you believe one of them's actually *boasting* about torching Chandra's flat?'

Hurrying after him, Catt and Shazia tried and failed to match the taller Casey's long and determined strides.

Eight

Fortunately, the two suspected arsonists had been picked up separately and kept apart, so had had no opportunity to regret earlier boasts and concoct alibis. And although, as it turned out, only one of the two youths had actually so far admitted to being responsible for the Bansi deaths, according to Sergeant Wright in the charge room even the more silent of the two hadn't denied their guilt.

Viewed through the hatches of their cell doors, Wayne Gough and Dean Linklater were like identikit pictures of the more thuggish young British male. From the 'No. 1' haircuts to the tattoos; from the expensive trainers to the sleeveless T-shirts and the Mr Macho muscular arms. Needless to say, they had both been in trouble before; for drunkenness, affray, general troublemaking.

According to Sergeant Wright, Wayne Gough had immediately demanded to see a solicitor. This loud demand had obviously been overheard by his pal, Linklater, in a cell two doors down, as it had been instantly repeated by him – as had further demands for a drink, food and cigarettes. 'Little Sir Echo' as Sergeant Wright called Linklater. 'Doesn't seem to have a thought to call his own.'

The demand for the brief at least had apparently only been for show, to make it clear they knew their rights. Because when the brief, who unfortunately happened to be Asian, arrived and Casey and Catt led him and his first client to one of the interview rooms, Wayne Gough gave him one sneering glance and then ignored him, told him to 'shut it' when he advised his unruly client to say nothing. Wayne wasn't going to be deprived of his moment of glory, certainly not by one of the 'enemy'.

Although Gough had already been cautioned, Casey cautioned him again for the benefit of the running tape. But it was evident that 'caution' wasn't a word in Wayne Gough's limited vocabulary. It quickly became clear that Gough was keen to boast of his brave deeds.

'Done 'em all, didn't we?' He sat back, stared contemptuously at his brief from eyes of indeterminate colour, before he folded his arms across his brawny chest and transferred his gaze to Casey. His eyes were empty of any emotion, though it was clear from the smug look that settled on his unshaven face that he felt he had done a good day's work. Gough's folded arms now concealed the abundant collection of showy rings that Casey had noticed earlier. They would serve admirably as a set of knuckledusters, the sizeable signet ring on his left ring finger being particularly eye-catching in both meanings of the word.

With a sneer, Gough rocked his chair on to its back legs and said, 'Paki bastards. Torch 'em out. Only way they'll go, innit?'

Casey wasn't a violent man but as, in his mind's eye, he saw again the appalling mortuary scenes he felt like punching Gough in his sneering, thin-lipped mouth. He breathed calmly, deeply, before he said, 'Let me get this clear. You're admitting you set fires at . . .' Casey glanced at his notebook and reeled off four addresses, including Chandra Bansi's.

Gough's brow wrinkled for a second as if he had trouble remembering – or reading – road names. Probably drunk at the time, Casey concluded.

Gough's brow cleared. He grinned and said, 'Yeah. That's right. Done 'em all. Quite a score.'

'The last one certainly was. You're a real hero, Wayne. We found the bodies of a young Asian woman and her nine-month-old baby in the last fire. Both died at the scene.'

He pulled the photograph of Chandra and her baby from his pocket. It had already been copied and circulated to the media. 'These are your victims.' He thrust the photograph under Gough's nose and told him, 'Take a good look. These are the human beings destroyed by your handiwork. Do you still feel proud of yourself?'

Gough directed one sneering glance at the photograph. But as Casey watched, the sneer disappeared and was replaced by bemusement. 'Hey, that's that bird . . .' he began before he broke off, sat back again and grinned smugly at them. 'Told the lads we did that one. Maybe now they'll believe us.'

Carefully, Casey returned the photograph to his pocket. Painstakingly, he took Gough through the arsons, extracting descriptions of the places torched, methods used and timings. Gough was confident enough about the earlier arson attacks and seemed to recall their circumstances pretty clearly. But when it came to the fire at Chandra's flat, he faltered, stumbling over his descriptions in a way that suggested he was now suffering after indulging in a lunchtime skinful, which, from the beer-tainted smell of his breath, seemed only too likely.

'Tell me again, Wayne,' Casey insisted. 'What accelerant did you use on the arson at Ainsley Terrace? How did you set it? At what time? Describe the street. Talk me through it.'

Gough crashed his chair back on all four of its legs and gazed belligerently at him. 'How many more times? You're giving me a bleedin' headache. I've told you we done it. What do you want me to go through all this rigmarole for?'

'You're the one keen to display his macho credentials, Wayne. All I want is to be sure your statement is an honest account of your claims and not simply conjured up to impress your mates.'

Casey's deliberate slur earned him a mouthful of colourful epithets. But it had the desired effect as Gough, reminded of his desire to impress his friends, tried harder. 'We used petrol, I suppose, like we usually do. Deano got it. It was lunchtime.

We'd been in the pub and had a skinful and decided we'd have a laugh and do another one.'

Catt prodded. 'So why did you choose those particular victims? Did you know the victim, Mrs Bansi?'

'Course not. Why would I know her?'

'I think what the sergeant is trying to understand is how you knew an Asian woman lived in the flat.'

'Oh that. We saw her, didn't we? Coupla days earlier. Gave us a load of lip. Saucy cow. So when we decided to do another one we settled on her. She got her comeuppance. Straight, she did.'

Casey began to experience some doubts that Gough was telling him the complete truth. Gough's earlier bemusement when he saw the picture of Chandra didn't indicate a prior knowledge of the victim's identity. Yet now he was claiming she had been selected *because* of prior knowledge. It made no sense. 'Mrs Bansi mentioned to her father that a couple of young men had harassed her a few days before her death. Are you saying that was you and Linklater?'

'Yeah. All we did was tell her to go back where she came from. Bitch told us we should go back to school and learn some manners. Bleedin' cheek. We taught her all right.'

'So how did you set the fire?'

Gough frowned, but the effort was too great. 'Can't remember. You're doin' my bleedin' head in with all these questions. Probably through the letterbox. That's how we done the other ones. You know, the old Indian rope trick. Soak some string in petrol, pour more through the letterbox, drop the other end of the string through and whoosh, up it goes.' He grinned.

Gough's solicitor, who had repeatedly tried to restrain his client, butted in again and got another mouthful of abuse for his trouble. Gough sat back, looking very pleased with himself.

When he recalled the recent scenes at the mortuary, Casey had to fight the lingering desire to punch the grin from

Wayne's face. Instead, ignoring the frisson of doubt increased by Gough's faulty recollections of Chandra's flat, he told him, 'You're going down for a long stretch, Wayne. I doubt you'll find your fellow prisoners quite as easy to intimidate as your victims.'

Wayne's bravado didn't falter. He was still on an adrenalin- and alcohol-fuelled high. And although they continued to press him to supply details, his memory grew more hazy rather than less. Finally, he clammed up and refused to answer any more of their questions. Casey told the attending uniformed officer to take him away and bring up his fellow suspect.

Alone for the moment as the duty solicitor had followed his client out, and as they waited for Dean Linklater to be brought up from the cells, Catt said, 'We'd better be sure he did all of them. Don't want him wriggling out and retracting his confession. He seemed pretty hazy on details of the Chandra arson.'

Casey gave a grim nod. There were other aspects of Gough's confession that jarred too. All the previous arsons amongst the Asian community had occurred at night, in the early hours. Typical after-pub mindless violence. But the fire at Chandra Bansi's flat had happened at lunchtime in the middle of a bright summer's day. There was the additional difference that the previous fires had been set via the letter-boxes rather than by gaining entry. And although the fire centre of the latest arson was in the back living room, Gough had seemed unaware of that, or been able to furnish them with any details or descriptions of the flat as he'd been able to do with the earlier cases. Gough's lack of knowledge bothered him.

'We need to be aboutely watertight on this one,' Casey commented. 'If we get them to court and they get off on some technicality, I'll never forgive myself. I promised Chandra's father I'd get the perpetrators. I mean to keep that promise.' As he heard the sounds of the other prisoner and his escort approaching along the corridor, Casey lowered his voice and added, 'We'll have another go at Gough later. Maybe when he's finished sobering up he'll remember a few more facts about it. If he's intent on incriminating himself, I want him to do a thorough job of it.'

In spite of his confident words, Casey couldn't shake off the shiver of doubt. Drunk or not, Gough's statement had been clear enough on the earlier arsons. Why should his memory of those be so much brighter than it was on the more recent one at Chandra's flat? It didn't make sense. He could only hope that Dean Linklater's memory proved more reliable.

Gough's accomplice was a similarly tough-looking macho man and sported an equally impressive selection of rings. Yet they were both unemployed. And as he wondered how they could afford them, Casey decided it would be a good idea to check out thefts from local jewellers.

Casey hoped again that Wayne Gough's faulty memory wasn't shared by his friend. If just one of the pair could recall significant details of the arson in Ainsley Terrace, he would be content that they *had* committed the fatal attack and could set about securing their conviction. And as he gazed into Dean Linklater's suspiciously moist pale blue eyes and gained the impression that in his case the toughness was no more than surface deep, Casey's faltering confidence began to return. Although at first Dean Linklater's bravado was every bit as showy as Gough's, Casey felt this suspect was the more likely of the two to yield to pressure and tell them the whole truth.

But in this, he was mistaken. Like Gough, Linklater ignored the caution and the same Asian solicitor and sat back, searching for and retrieving some of his slowly trickling cockiness. 'You should've seen those bastards when they watched their places go up in smoke,' he bragged. 'We hung about so we could watch. Screamin' and cryin' and throwing their arms about, they were. Right laugh.'

With difficulty, Casey kept his voice and expression neutral. 'So you'd think it funny if everything *you* owned went up in smoke, would you?' he asked softly. 'All your clothes with their designer labels, your expensive trainers and your music collection.'

Dean's eyes narrowed. 'What you talkin' about? They're Pakis. They're not into stuff like that – wear sandals and saris or suits, don't they? Gawd knows what they listen to – that wailing stuff probably. Better burnt.'

'The older generation of Asians, just like the older generation of English, might not be into modern western fashion and music,' Casey conceded. 'But the younger ones are into the same things as you, Dean.' Casey wondered why he was bothering to try to instill a feeling of shame, of remorse; if he and Gough had deliberately set the fires he was likely to be incapable of either emotion. But he persevered. 'And your victims were British-born Indians, not Pakistanis.' Not that it made any difference to Linklater and his charmless friend. 'You've got more in common than you think. The young man whose flat you torched last week is in a band.'

'Yeah, right. A wailing band, right?' Dean sneered.

'The band's pretty catholic in its taste, I understand. Rock, hip-hop, garage. You should see their stage gear. All slashed leather and chains.' Casey had been told this by one of his younger colleagues. At the age of thirty-five, he had not only long since given up attending such concerts, he had never started. 'Luckily, their stage stuff and instruments had been left overnight in their van so it didn't go up with the young man's flat. At least he can still earn a living.'

Dean stared at him, the macho pose suddenly forgotten. 'What you sayin'? That he plays in a *real* band. He actually makes a living from gigs?' Clearly some, at least, of Dean's beliefs about the alien nature of the Asian community were being stood on their head. From where Casey was sitting it looked an uncomfortable experience.

'One of my younger colleagues went to see them play at the local college last month. He raved about them. Said they're going places.'

Dean's mouth hung open. Gobsmacked, Casey concluded. And well he might be. Dean's mother – the would-be Mr Macho still lived at home – had told uniformed officers that Dean had musical aspirations himself, though he was apparently finding mastery of the guitar more demanding than fire-setting.

Once Dean had digested the fact that one of his Asian victims was so far from being alien as to share his musical ambitions, he became subdued. He slumped back in his chair and some of his machismo melted away. Here was something he could relate to.

He became even more subdued as they brought the questioning around to the latest, fatal arson and sat hunched and miserable under their questions.

'I suppose Wayne confessed to that one, too?' he finally asked.

'Yes,' Casey told him. 'His solicitor couldn't get him to shut up. Wayne couldn't get the words out quick enough. He also implicated you.'

Linklater merely nodded as though he had been expecting this. And as it gradually dawned on him what a bleak future awaited him, a look of desperation entered his eyes. He gazed from Casey to Catt, to his solicitor and back again, his gaze flickering from face to face as though searching for a way out. Several times his lips opened as if he was going to speak, maybe even deny his part in the killings, but each time his eyes shadowed and he closed them again.

Finally, he seemed to accept his fate and, his voice sounding like that of an automaton, said dully, 'Yeah, we did it. Me and Wayne. Can I go back to my cell now? I feel sick.'

'There's a bucket in the corner,' Casey told him bluntly. 'I suggest you make use of that if you need to throw up.' He had brought it in anticipating that one of their sobering suspects might need to vomit. The interview room was basic, its grimy decor unlikely to be improved by vomit. Besides, he didn't see why the cleaners' task should be made even more unpleasant by the likes of Dean Linklater. 'We'll need some details.'

Dean looked blankly at him. 'Details? What do you mean? I don't know no details. We done it, that's all I know. Wayne's the details man.'

And although they worked hard to get concrete evidence from him on the Bansi arson, Linklater's memory proved poorer than Gough's. Interspersed with groans as he periodically vomited the contents of his stomach into the plastic bucket, he claimed to be unable to remember anything and, in answer to their questions, moaned, 'Ask Wayne. He'll know.'

He couldn't even remember where he'd bought – or more probably stolen – the petrol Gough claimed they had used to set the fire. Casey had earlier ordered his teams to check out the local filling stations and play their security videos, but their two suspects hadn't featured on any of them. Of course, they could have got the petrol further afield, but why would they go to the trouble when neither denied their guilt?

Like Wayne Gough, Linklater soon tired of their persistant probing. Unable or unwilling to tell them any more, it was at least in his favour that he lacked his friend's eager desire to boast of their achievements. Instead, he sat sullen and miserable, hunched over the now foul-smelling bucket. Eventually, when Casey produced the photograph of Chandra and Leela, he took refuge in silence. And although he apparently retained sufficient sense of shame to flush as he gazed at the picture, he also had the sense to finally take notice of his solicitor, and he volunteered nothing further.

Now that his adopted swagger – which Casey suspected was put on in imitation of his pal – had melted away, the real Dean was clearly seen. He looked terrified, though whether his terror was in anticipation of what he could expect in prison, or from the retribution his friend would mete out if he attempted to save his own skin and backtrack on his admission of guilt, wasn't clear.

Weak, painfully immature and easily led, Casey could believe that 'Little Sir Echo' had followed, sheep-like, behind Gough's evil lead, too much under his brash friend's influence to develop a mind or a life of his own. And although every bit as guilty as his friend, Linklater still retained sufficient decency to have a sense of shame, as his ugly flush had revealed. Without the older Gough's Svengali-like influence, Linklater might have had a chance to grow into a decent human being. Of course, if the case went to court and they were found guilty, they would both go down. But that was a long way in the future. And far from certain, even after the two confessions.

That neither of them could supply convincing details worried him. His only hope was that a night's sleep would encourage the return of memory.

Casey suggested to Dean that it was long past time he started thinking for himself. He was old enough to take responsibility for his actions. Old enough, too, to decide for himself what those actions should be.

Linklater glanced at him but said nothing. Though from the way Dean was biting his lip as he was led away, Casey thought something had got through.

Superintendent Brown-Smith was jubilant. He even went so far as to clap Casey on the back and tell him, 'Well done.'

Casey managed an uneasy smile. He tried to explain his misgivings to the superintendent, but Brown-Smith brushed them aside. 'They were both drunk out of their trees,' he said. 'Of course they're going to be vague on details. What else can you expect with scum like that?'

Casey's doubts made him persist. 'I'd like a little more time to investigate their movements before I charge them. Even if these two idiots can't remember details they might have boasted of them to their friends before drink drowned their memories. I know you'll want this case to be as solid as I can make it.'

Brown-Smith's button-brown gaze narrowed as if he suspected Casey was trying to delay or even deny him the congratulatory laurels that were probably already resounding in his head. But he hadn't reached the rank of superintendent by not covering all the bases and now he said, 'Very well. Check them out by all means. As you said, we want no mistakes on this one. I'll arrange an extension to their detention period to give you the time.'

Casey nodded. Unfortunately, in spite of Brown-Smith's confidence, Casey didn't feel as certain as the superintendent that the investigation was concluded. And although neither Gough nor Linklater had retracted their statements once they had sobered up, they had both become very quiet.

Casey had set Catt to finding and questioning their families and friends – a racially non-sensitive area to which even Brown–Smith could have no objection – conscious that in spite of his brushing aside of Casey's anxieties, the superintendent would recall them all too readily if the prosecution failed and he would blame Casey for not pressing his point more strongly.

Nine

The inquest on Chandra and Leela Bansi was opened the next morning. Casey, as investigating officer, attended. He was accompanied by Superintendent Brown-Smith. Of the family, only Rathi Khan and his son, Devdan, attended. Casey had intended to speak to them but the opportunity didn't present itself, as they slipped away quietly from another exit before he had the chance.

The press was there en masse and managed to turn what should have been a solemn, formal occasion into something of a scrum. Thankfully, the inquest was simply a formality and had been quickly adjourned pending further enquiries.

Afterwards, on the steps of the coroner's court, Brown-Smith spoke to the assembled media. He took the opportunity to criticize irresponsible journalism. His words were carefully chosen, moderate and designed to impress those with police promotion in their gift; this was Brown-Smith's public face. Public relations was something he excelled at. Casey often thought he would have made a superb politician – not because he would be likely to achieve anything worthwhile – but because, like any politician with ambitions for high office, he could spin truth on its head and come out sounding both sincere and honest. It was quite a skill – one Casey had never mastered.

Brown-Smith was careful not to mention Gwyn Owen, the local newspaperman, and his speculative article, and he spoke more in sorrow than anger. Casey guessed he was still seething about it inside but anger was reserved for his other face, the one presumably only his family and lower-ranking officers like Casey ever saw.

Casey, conscious of his promise to Brown-Smith, had been sure to keep Thomas Catt well away from the proceedings. He had sent him off with DC Jim Heron to continue his attempts at interviewing Gough and Linklater's friends and family. Their friends, at least, had so far proved elusive. For some reason they weren't keen to speak to the police. But too much was riding on these interviews, and although Casey would have preferred to go with Catt himself, he had to attend the inquest, and time and the superintendent were pressing. He had told Catt, if he managed to find one of their elusive interviewees, to take as long as he needed, but to come back with some answers.

Back in the office later that morning, Casey concentrated on working his way through the many reports. Unfortunately, they added little to the sum of his knowledge. By the time he had finished the afternoon was rapidly drawing on to evening.

Catt stuck his glossy head round the door of Casey's office just as the phone rang. Casey waved him to a chair as he picked up the phone.

'That was the lab,' he told Catt when he put the phone down five minutes later. 'The gas chromatography tests on the debris at Chandra's flat confirm the presence of an accelerant. Petrol.'

The report confirmed what they had already suspected.

'They also found several tiny pieces of some red material. The twisted metals they found strewn about were pieces of jewellery – rings and bangles, apparently.'

'Strange they weren't on the body,' said Catt.

'Chandra was a widow, remember. According to Shazia Singh, Hindu widows aren't supposed to wear jewellery.'

'But Chandra was a modern girl, westernized. Would she have taken notice of such old-fashioned restrictions? Particularly when she was alone.'

Casey shrugged. 'Whether she would or not she wasn't actually *wearing* any jewellery when she was found. These rings and bangles and so on, which is what the lab believes them to be, were just lying on the floor. Perhaps she was just having a trying-on session to cheer herself up.'

Catt threw another idea into the ring. 'Maybe this was a burglary gone wrong. You saw what a collection of rings our two heroes, Gough and Linklater, wore. Maybe Chandra disturbed them as they were burgling the place and they committed double murder and arson as a panic measure.'

'What, you mean this was their night for burgling and they brought petrol with them as a just-in-case measure?'

'Put like that, it does sound unlikely,' Catt admitted. 'Unless they thumped her unconscious, went off to buy petrol and returned to finish the job. That way they'd get to do two of their favourite things at once.'

They looked at one another. It was a possibility, one that hadn't previously occurred to Casey, though whether Gough and Linklater were the burglars . . .

'So how did you get on? Did you manage to find any of Gough or Linklater's friends? If you did, it's clear from your comments that you didn't get anything concrete.'

Catt shook his head. 'I finally managed to track down Wayne Gough's girlfriend. Sullen madam by the name of Tara Tompkins. Told me what sounded like a pack of lies. According to her, Gough was with her, not Linklater, at the time of the fire at Chandra's flat. She turned sullen when I asked her to prove it and refused to say more, apart from claiming a local vicar as a witness.' Catt scoffed. 'A likely story. Can you see our friend Gough hobnobbing with vicars?'

It sounded pretty unlikely, Casey admitted. 'Though the fact that she didn't come up with something more believable makes me think she could be telling the truth. Unless she's stupid she must realize we'd find it hard to swallow such a tale. Shame she clammed up. Maybe she only told you half a tale because she's scared that Gough would take exception. He wouldn't like his girlfriend trying to protect him when it exposes him as a liar to his mates.'

Catt nodded. 'I can imagine he'd be handy with his fists. Anyway, I tried contacting this vicar, but he's away at present, so I wasn't able to get her story substantiated one way or the other. I left a message for the vicar to contact us on his return.'

Casey nodded. And although Catt was still inclined to think it was a waste of time, Casey wasn't so sure. If what the girl claimed was true, it would not only make Gough's confession worthless as far as the Chandra Bansi case was concerned, it would probably mean that Linklater's was too. Casey couldn't see Linklater having the nerve to fire-set without the bolstering bravado of Gough.

But until this vicar returned they would have to bear their impatience for answers as well as they could. And it wasn't as if he hadn't been half-expecting something of the sort ever since he'd listened to their confessions. Dryly he asked, 'Will you tell the superintendent or shall I?'

'You, I think,' Catt replied. 'Privileges of rank, and all that.'

Casey nodded. 'But not just yet. Like us, the superintendent can wait upon the vicar's return.'

' "Sufficient unto the day is the evil thereof"?' Catt mocked.

'No. Merely that until we've something definite to tell him there's no point. You know as well as I do that he prefers things clear-cut.' Casey sat and stared thoughtfully into space. In spite of his reasoned arguments concerning the jewellery, after what Catt had told him he now had even more reason to doubt Gough and Linklater's involvement. There was some niggling aspect of that scenario that jarred with him, something he couldn't quite put his finger on. Just because Gough, at least, had been so keen to claim the Bansi arson was no reason for him to believe the two were involved. It wasn't as if their claimed recollections of the act were clear. It wasn't even as if the Bansi arson bore the same MO as the earlier ones.

And then there was the matter of the baby, little Leela. The toxicology reports revealed the presence of drugs in the child. A large quantity of a sleeping draught, enough to knock such a small baby right out, and very quickly. He told Catt about it.

Catt had a perfectly reasonable explanation. 'The baby was a bawler. We already knew that. What could be more understandable than for Chandra, who sounded like she had plenty of reasons to be at the end of her tether, to just dope the kid up to the eyeballs so she could get some rest?'

'It's a possibility, of course. But no matter how tired, would a responsible mother give her child such a large quantity of drugs? According to the toxicology report, it was perilously close to a fatal dose.'

Always ready with suggestions, Catt put forward another one. 'It would make sense if Chandra had already decided to kill herself in the classic sati manner and take the baby with her, but didn't want the child to suffer. That would explain the drugs. It would also explain the fact that this one has a different MO. You already had plenty of doubts of our two suspects' involvement. What if this turns out not to be murder at all? Or rather, a murder and suicide, by Chandra herself. Who could blame her if she had decided she and her baby were better off dead? It was what her brother implied, after all. The girl's future sounded bleak. Sure, she could have refused to remarry, moved away and found herself a partner outside the Hindu community. But if she did that her family might have disowned her or set bounty hunters on her to punish her for dishonouring the family. Besides, in that scenario her child came into the equation. Would Chandra condemn her daughter to an outlawed existence? With a mother always looking over her shoulder and obliged for her own safety never to see her family again? The other alternative, of agreeing to accept the partner her father found for her, however unsuitable, was scarcely an improvement. She had already had one bad experience of marriage, of living with in-laws. Would she really have wanted to risk repeating it, particularly as Leela, too, might end up mistreated? And if, as Dan Khan suggested, it was an elderly husband in India her father was trying for, she would be isolated, far from her family. The poor girl would have been in a fix whatever course she decided upon.'

Casey nodded. As usual, Catt had set out the facts plainly. Too plainly. With anyone else in such a position, Casey would think that infanticide followed by suicide was a strong possibility. But, despite the theory Catt had put forward so persuasively, Casey wasn't convinced. From all he had learned of Chandra he didn't feel that suicide would be her natural choice. She had been strong, vivacious, not lacking in either confidence or courage. Even if she had been in a state of depression, it would surely have been a temporary thing only. After all, she had been a beautiful young woman. Casey couldn't conceive of any young woman choosing to destroy her beauty and that of her little daughter.

And even if she *had* chosen death, there were so many alternatives. In spite of what he had learned from Shazia Singh, he felt that such a death would never figure highly on anyone's list of suicide choices.

Casey sat back with a sigh. They had a long way to go yet. Theorizing was all very well, but proof was better and they had little enough of that so far. Conscious that the hour of his daily tête-à-tête with Superintendent Brown-Smith was again approaching, he wanted something to give him, and now he questioned Catt again. 'Did you manage to track down any of Gough and Linklater's other friends?'

Catt shook his head. Unsurprisingly, their friends had proved evasive, Gough had no close family. Linklater's mother – the father had long since left home – insisted her son was innocent, though as she had been at work at the time of the arson she was unable to substantiate her claims. Unlike Gough, Linklater had no girlfriend. Their only hopes of getting anything to confirm or negate the confessions were Gough's girlfriend and this missing vicar.

Already tired from absorbing the vast quantity of paperwork the team had produced, his theorizing with Catt had made his head spin. He felt stale and not in any state to conduct an important interview, so perhaps it was just as well no one but the super was eager to talk to him.

What he needed – what they both needed – was a break, and now Casey proposed an early night and a few beers. Starting the next day refreshed might be the best way to move on with the investigation.

He was surprised when Catt agreed. Although his sergeant lived alone, his evenings were normally taken up with a veritable harem of ladyfriends. Casey had a theory that Catt's large number of girlfriends was a self-protection device designed to prevent any one of them getting serious and expecting commitment. After his abandonment as a toddler and subsequent upbringing in several children's homes, Thomas Catt was naturally wary of commitment, of putting his emotional happiness into another's hands. But Casey believed that, in spite of evidence to the contrary, Thom secretly longed for a secure family life if only he could overcome his fear of abandonment.

After Superintendent Brown-Smith had wrung what remained of Casey's energy from him, he and Catt adjourned to The Lamb. The Lamb, now called The Rat and Parrot, much to Casey's disgust, was always referred to by them by its earlier name. Situated in the centre of the town, it was a busy pub with a surprisingly wide menu. An additional attraction was its large garden – situated by the river and shaded by several large weeping willows, it was perfect for summer evenings.

Maybe, Casey thought as he sat slumped in the garden waiting for Catt to return from the bar, the combination of a few beers followed by an early night would help shake loose the little niggle that had taken root in his brain. Besides, the interview with Chandra's in-laws, Mr and Mrs Bansi, was arranged for the next day and Casey had a feeling that he might need a good night's sleep before he tackled those particular suspects.

'By the way, said Catt as he returned, handed Casey his pint and sat down opposite him in the pub's garden, 'have you got squatters?'

'Squatters? What do you mean?'

'It's just that I passed your house earlier and saw this bedraggled old bloke coming out of your front door. I was about to challenge him, but then the radio went and I had to leave. Forgot about it till now.'

Casey hadn't confided his parental problems to Catt. Now he thought as quickly as his tired brain would allow and said, 'Must have been my father. I've got my parents staying for a few days,' he explained. 'My father offered to do a bit of gardening while he's here. No doubt he had on his disreputable old gardening clothes. Makes him look like a superannuated hippie.'

Catt laughed. 'That's all right, then. Just as well I didn't challenge him.' Catt's voice grew wistful. 'Must be nice having your parents visiting. God knows where mine are. They could be dead for all I know.'

'Have you never thought of trying to trace them?' Casey asked, keen to get off the subject of his own parents.

Catt shook his head. 'What's the point? They didn't want me when I was a toddler so they're unlikely to want me now.' Abruptly, he changed the subject. 'So, tell me about your parents. What do they do? Where do they live? I'm surprised you've never mentioned them.'

Casey had never mentioned them for several very good reasons, one of which was that it seemed insensitive to talk about one's parents with Thom. 'They've got a smallholding,' he said. 'Miles away in the Fens.'

'Must have been fun growing up there with animals and tractors and a barn to play in,' said Thom, sounding even more wistful. 'Sounds idyllic.'

Casey gave a wry smile, but didn't disabuse Thom of the notion that his childhood had been idyllic. Why disillusion him? Instead he nodded at Catt's nearly empty pint and said,

101

'Fancy another?' Keen to get off the subject of parents, Casey added, 'I wanted to discuss how I'm going to handle tomorrow's interview. You can think about it while I get the drinks in. One more won't put us over the limit.'

Later that evening, home early for once, Casey decided he would be wise to listen to his doubts about Gough and Linklater's complicity in the Bansi deaths. If they proved well founded he would need to consider other suspects, so he might as well start now. It was probably time he learned something more about Asians and their culture in any case, especially as the next day would bring the interview with Mr and Mrs Bansi.

So, after dinner that evening, Casey asked his mother about her experiences of India. Shazia Singh had reminded him of things he had mostly forgotten; if he had ever known them at all.

Stretched out on a cushion, head in hands in the flickering candlelight which his mother preferred, she looked young again. He noticed she still wore the little carving of the Hindu elephant god, Ganesh, on a cord round her neck. It was his mother's prized possession, having been given to her by a sadhu, one of India's many wandering holy men.

In popular Hinduism, Ganesh was, he recalled, an important god. As his mother had told him many times, in an attempt to spark his interest in Indian mysticism, as a policeman he should be grateful for any help received and Ganesh was supposed to be the remover of obstacles. He was prayed to by Hindus before any important event, whether it was getting married, moving house or taking examinations. The son of the great god Shiva, Ganesh or Ganesha had had his head struck off by Shiva after Parvati, his mother, had asked her son to mount sentry outside her room and permit no one to enter. To the boy, his mother's explicit instructions clearly included his father and, after various failed attempts to gain entry to Parvati's room, Shiva had finally struck the boy's head off with his trident. At Parvati's insistence, Shiva replaced the boy's head with the head of the first living being he met, which happened to be an elephant.

Casey could only be thankful that the fiercely tusked carving had not pierced *his* flesh during his mother's hug of greeting.

There was a piece of her 'wailing' music playing softly in the background. With the candlelight and the burning sandalwood joss sticks his mother favoured delicately perfuming his living room, if he half-closed his eyes and fixed them on a particular part of his prized scripophily collection – a framed old share certificate of the India General Navigation and Railway Company with its river boat and onion-domed building in the background – they might almost be back in India. To complete his memories of that time, his father was stretched out on the floor with his head in his mother's lap, snoring softly.

Invited to talk about her favourite subject, his mother smiled. 'What do you want to know?'

'Anything. Everything.'

She gave a low chuckle. 'Silly Willy. I can't tell you *everything*. No one knows that. India is a country of many mysteries, much spirituality, great kindness and great cruelty, too. Many different peoples, languages, religions, history. The contrasts are, like, way out.'

Smarting a little under his mother's 'Silly Willy' tag, he said shortly, 'I know that much.' He had been there, after all. 'I meant tell me something more specific. For instance, someone was telling me about widows today. What an awful time they have of it. Is it true?'

She nodded. 'I don't know what you've heard, but I expect so. We were there in '87 when another case of widow-burning hit the headlines. Young woman, not even out of her teens. Only been married a matter of months. There was speculation that she hadn't climbed on the pyre willingly.'

Casey hunched forward encouragingly as his mother

paused, as if she had trouble recalling the past through the haze of drugs she had consumed in between. 'Go on.'

'Give me a chance, Willow.' His mother sat up and eased another cushion under her legs where the weight of her husband's head pressed her into the floor. Her expression turned sombre. And as she spoke, it was evident her memories of that time were very clear. 'We'd been bumming around Rajasthan for a couple of weeks and hey – it was so in-your-face. All the local papers were full of this young woman's sati. The English-language rags followed suit. They raged about it for weeks as though such happenings were unheard of. But we got talking to another traveller – one who'd put down roots – and he told us that widow- and bride-burning caused regular uproar, although bride-burning was frequently disguised as kitchen accidents, and the widows were apparently always willing. Sounds barbaric, I know, but sati has a long history in the state. You've got to remember the centuries of violence and upheaval that brought it about. This guy – Seth, his name was – told us that the practice of sati went back at least to the times of the Moghul invasions when the infamous Chittor mass satis in Rajasthan occurred. The—'

'Hold on,' Casey interrupted. 'Tell me about the Chittor thing.'

'According to Seth, Rajputs had a code of chivalry and honour, something similar to the code of chivalry followed by our medieval knights. When they were invaded, even when they were massively outnumbered, rather than doing the sensible thing and retreating to fight another day, their code of honour demanded they don saffron robes and ride out to meet death on the battlefield. Meanwhile, so that they wouldn't be dishonoured in the usual fashion by the invading army, this same code demanded that their women and children commit *jauhar* – mass suicide – on huge funeral pyres. A relatively quick death by fire was considered to be the better option than the dishonour and inevitable death following multiple rape. Among Rajputs, honour was always more important than death.'

His father stirred in his sleep, grunted and turned over. 'So what numbers are we talking about here?' Casey asked.

'Patience, Willow. Let me tell you in my own way. Where was I? Oh yes. Mass suicide happened three times in Chittorgarh's long history, the last one was sometime in the sixteenth century. During the previous invasion, when the fort was again besieged, Seth told us that around 13,000 Rajput women and 32,000 warriors died after the declaration of *jauhar*.'

Casey let out a long, low whistle at this and muttered, 'Jesus.'

'As with so many traditions, sati clung on, particularly among the illiterate peasants.'

Casey sat back as he tried to imagine the scene at one of these *jauhars*. Fortunately, his mind was unable or unwilling to compose the horrific pictures necessary.

The story had obviously made a deep and lasting impression on his mother for her to recall it so vividly and with such ease. How the uneducated clung to well-worn ways, even when the need for them had long passed. Casey remembered his great-grandmother, his mother's gran. A countrywoman, born and bred in the East Anglian Fens, she had religiously followed the practices she had learnt in her youth – of force-feeding Casey senna to give him 'a good clearout'; of smothering his chest in goose grease whenever he had a sniffle, covering it with brown paper and then applying an iron; of wringing the necks of chickens without a qualm. Substitute women for chickens and fire for neck-wringing and it was easy to see that the way things had always been done could so easily continue without anyone questioning them. There were enough examples in British history of men riding out valiantly towards almost certain death; 'The Charge of the Light Brigade' and going over the top in the First World War were just two. With his interest in history, which had sparked the start of his scripophily collection, Casey was aware that in Britain's past, death had been cheap, much as it was in present-day India and other parts of the Third World. Change was a thing that happened slowly, as leaders such as the Shah of Iran and Rajiv Ghandi had learned to their cost.

He gestured for his mother to continue and she resumed her story. 'For Rajputs, the death of a widow on her husband's pyre was regarded as the equal in courage to that of a Rajput warrior dying on the battlefield. It's like a glory thing. Hey, these guys have got temples dedicated to sati all over the state. There's bread in it. In some places the entire economy is dependent on visitors to the local temple spending their dosh. Widows might be outcasts, but once they're burned they become deities. You should see some of the temples. Seth took us to one at Kotri, the Sati Savitri temple, which was built in memory of a woman named Savitri who was im-molated on her husband's pyre.' She frowned. 'On April the first, nineteen seventy-three if I remember rightly.'

'Bit extreme for an April Fool's jape.'

'There's nothing funny about a fundamentalist Hindu guy caught up in some religious rite. There was a kind of altar at this temple. It had a woman's figure with a triangular brass head and a *ghagra*, an image of Durga, a female deity, astride a lion.' She frowned. 'Let's see if I can remember this right – it's been a long time. The dead woman apparently acquires the *shakti* – the energy or lifeforce, I suppose – of Durga, who enters her and becomes the *sati mata*; a new, powerful goddess embodied in the two-eyed trishul. The two-eyed trishul re-presents the,' she shrugged faintly, 'metamorphosis, I sup-pose, of the woman Savitri into the goddess *sati mata* Savitri Devi.'

'Not much consolation in becoming a goddess when you're reduced to ashes.'

'That's what I said, but some of the Indian women I spoke to told me that Rajput females are amongst the most sub-jugated in the country. Few get any schooling. Once you become a widow there your life's over. Widows bring such bad karma that the general drift I got from the women was that it was better for them to be a dead goddess than a living outcast. Many thought climbing on the fire would win out every time over a lingering living death. Strange country. Fascinating, too. You should go there.' She smiled. 'Might loosen you up.'

Funny, thought Casey, but his mother seemed to have forgotten that he *had* been to India, much as she and his father had forgotten about him for days at a time when as a child he had accompanied them on the hippie trail. Probably, all the drugs she had taken down the years had damaged her memory. Or maybe it had always been selective. And if she forgot he was there, she could also forget how she and his father had left him to fend for himself.

'The contrasts are, like, way out,' she went on when he didn't speak. 'Barbaric practices like widow- and bride-burning on the one hand, and a terrific growth in the hi-tech industry on the other.'

Casey nodded. He had read in the paper only the other day that lots of British firms subcontracted IT work to India. Not only were they world-class in the field, their computer nerds were also far cheaper than England's.

As his mother said – a strange, fascinating land, vast and sprawling, full of contrasts such as modern hi-tech alongside barbaric medieval ritual.

And, as he went to bed later that night, Casey's only hope was that his doubts about Gough and Linklater's guilt were unfounded. Because if they weren't, he would have to start investigating the Khan and Bansi families' possible complicity in Chandra and Leela's deaths. And after what his mother had told him, he wasn't sure he had the stomach for the further delving into India's culture that such an investigation would require.

Ten

M r and Mrs Sanjit and Roop Bansi lived in a three-bedroomed semi on the outskirts of King's Langley. The house would have been spacious but for all the clutter. Casey wondered whether their home was used as an extension to their business storeroom, as all sorts of Indian artefacts and materials seemed to be stacked around the house. He recognized several *pitaras*, traditional carved wooden chests, dotted around the room. The chests had small doors in front which, as he remembered from Indian folklore, were designed to deter thieves from stealing too many items from the chest at any one time. These were no doubt considered good enough for the export market, but as he recalled, they were far inferior to the magnificent examples of wood artistry he had seen in some of the palaces in India.

On top of the chests were piled bolts of fabric; mirrored Rajasthani embroidery, hand-worked *salma* saris. Another pile contained crewel-worked *toran* wall and door hangings. In the corner was a teetering pile of beautifully detailed *jali* carvings.

Every wall was covered in pictures of a young man in his early twenties, whom Casey took to be the dead son, Magan. The pictures portrayed a good-looking, self-confident young man, verging on the podgy; the only-son-syndrome mentioned by Angela Neerey clearly evident in the well-fed cheeks and self-satisfied expression.

The quantity of photos of him indicated that the son now ranked amongst the Indian gods in his mother's eyes, statues of which cluttered every flat surface not already occupied, and which had apparently spread out from the corner shrine. Casey remembered several of them: Ganesh, of course, the popular elephant god, his mother's particular favourite, Krishna, with his crown of peacock feathers; Brahma, Vishnu and Shiva, the *Trimurti*.

On the sofa, looking like a particularly well-fed Buddha, sat Mrs Bansi with her husband squashed into a tiny corner beside her. Hard not to be reminded of Jack Spratt and his wife, was Casey's thought. Mr Bansi was as thin as a bean-pole, with a cadaverous face and desiccated-looking skin, a bundle of twigs only held together by his clothing. She appeared as wide as she was high, with pendulous jowls that wobbled in tandem with the loose skin under her upper arms. She reminded Casey of the first – and only – children's party he had attended, at the age of five, when he had seen a jelly for the first time – his hippie mother not being given to the provision of puddings – and had been so fascinated by the wondrous wobbling propensity of the jelly that his attempts to make it wobble still further had caused it to wobble to the floor. He had never forgotten it or the swift slap his friend's harassed mother had administered; the injustice still rankled.

There seemed no danger of the jelly woman collapsing to her carpet. Mrs Bansi looked as firmly set on the bright orange floral settee as Queen Victoria had on her throne. Her voice was shrill and easily overpowered her husband's low tones. She certainly seemed the more dominant personality.

Casey was thankful the couple both spoke English; he had half-expected them to plead ignorance of the language in order to avoid his questioning. Perhaps they might have, but presumably they had realized that the presence of the uniformed Shazia Singh precluded such a stratagem.

Casey began by asking about their dead son and offering his condolences.

This set Mrs Bansi off. 'My beautiful boy. What a loss to a mother. And to lose such a one because of a *randi*.' Beside him, he heard the Asian WPC's swift, indrawn breath. But before Casey could glance at her, Mrs Bansi had clasped her beringed hands to her mighty bosom with such force that every bit of her began to wobble alarmingly; he almost expected bits of her to shoot off in all directions and go splat on the carpet. 'Such a good boy.' Wobble. 'Such a hard worker.' Wobble. 'How could you know what a loss my son is to me?' Wobble. 'Who will now look after me in my dotage?' Wobble, wobble.

Casey dragged his gaze from the human jelly to glance at the jelly's husband. He had scarcely uttered a word. At any moment Casey expected him to vanish altogether, his dry-kindling body crushed to dust by the exuberant exertions of his wife. She had made no mention of her husband's loss, or of Chandra's. Her words indicated that she did indeed blame Chandra for her son's death, however unjustly. Grief such as Mrs Bansi's didn't allow for mercy, or even fairness. Such grief and outraged passion in a mind as strong as Roop Bansi's could be a dangerous combination, particularly as ThomCatt, with a speed and initiative that Casey had come to expect, had somehow managed to uncover the information that Chandra would, indeed, have received a healthy inheritance from her late husband. A share of the business had been given to the son as a wedding gift and, as his widow, Chandra would have inherited under the intestacy laws, always presuming that her youthful husband had made no will.

Casey didn't think such a situation would have suited Roop Bansi. He suspected that Chandra would have needed to recruit an entire courtful of lawyers to get what was rightfully hers. From the little he had seen so far, he judged Roop Bansi capable of killing; her only difficulty would be finding the energy to heave her bulk from the sofa.

But there were two sides to every story and now, in an attempt to right the balance, Casey said, 'I understood your son, Magan, died in a car accident?'

Roop Bansi's small brown eyes were sunk into the flesh of her face, but still he couldn't mistake the glint of malevolence in their kohl-ringed depths. 'So? It was an accident that wouldn't have happened if he hadn't been driving that lazy wife of his to the shops to spend more of our money.'

Casey nodded. Now he understood at least part of the cause of Mrs Bansi's anger. As both Catt and Shazia Singh had remarked, so many murders came down to money in the end. No doubt she had resented every penny spent by Chandra's apparently besotted husband. At the risk of setting the jelly flesh wobbling again, he asked, 'You didn't approve of your son's wife?'

She made a pshawing sound. 'Approve, disapprove. She was not the girl she had been made out to be.' She gave her husband a reproachful glance before turning back to Casey. 'My husband arranged the marriage. He and Mr Khan are business acquaintances.'

'Partners, now,' her husband murmured beside her. 'Since the marriage.'

Mrs Bansi gave a less than delicate snort at this interruption and continued her condemnation of her daughter-in-law. 'Even before the marriage I thought her too modern, too opinionated, too given to Western ideas and the wearing of Western clothes. I did my best to put a stop to *that* once they were married. A girl should be submissive to her husband's parents.'

Casey guessed that only one person in this house was entitled to voice opinions. It certainly wasn't her husband, who seemed cowed by his forceful wife. He was surprised that Sanjit Bansi had been permitted to arrange the son's wedding. But perhaps that, too, had come down to money. Financially, at least on the surface, Mr Bansi had made a good match for his son. No doubt that had appealed to Mrs Bansi at the time, which was why he had been allowed to get on with it. But maybe, as with the bride, doubts as to the bargain made had begun to set in. It was only now, when all

111

their hopes and dreams of the future affluence that should have flowed from the families' union had ended, that she voiced her reproaches.

It was interesting to learn the men were business partners. Surely it would have provided Mr Bansi – or his wife – with ample opportunity to get hold of the keys to Chandra's flat and have them copied? They were even conveniently marked 'Flat – front door' and 'Flat – back door', as he had noticed when Rathi Khan had fumbled his car keys from the ring.

But Mrs Bansi's hearty condemnation of her dead daughter-in-law wasn't indicative of guilt in her death; rather the opposite. Unless, of course, even the need for self-preservation was unable to curb her tongue.

He guessed that, in Chandra, Mrs Bansi had got more than she had bargained for. She would have found her vivacious, westernised daughter-in-law no mean opponent. Chandra wouldn't have let herself be crushed by this weighty human jelly without putting up a fight.

Determined not to be crushed himself, Casey addressed his next remark to Mr Bansi. 'And what about you, sir? How did you feel about Chandra?'

Before he had a chance to open his mouth, his wife answered for him. 'What should he feel? I tell you the girl was not the good bargain she had been held up to be. Her extravagance would have beggared us all in time. These young, westernized Asian women are all the same. None of them concern themselves with their duties. It is always the laughing and joking with them.'

Casey thought it unlikely that Chandra would have had much opportunity for light-hearted behaviour in this house. Of course, he must remember they had lost their only son, a greatly beloved son if the number of photographs were any indication. But their personalities had been formed long before their son's death. Mr Bansi wore the anxious look of one habitually in the wrong. Mrs Bansi's voice and manner were those of a bully who had had years to perfect her art.

She opened her mouth and was evidently about to begin another tirade when her husband muttered something under his breath. Her gaze darted from Casey to Shazia Singh and back again and the expected tirade remained unspoken. Instead, she asked, 'What for you are asking us these questions? She is dead and good riddance, but we had nothing to do with it. It is not for you to cross-question us when we are weak from grief from the loss of our son.'

Mr Bansi was apparently not quite as ineffective as he appeared, for now he broke in. 'My wife is distraught, Inspector. She doesn't understand what she is saying.'

Casey reminded himself that although Sanjit Bansi seemed a meek creature in the presence of his wife, he must be fairly shrewd as he ran what was, by all accounts, a very successful and profitable business importing traditional Indian artefacts, which found a ready market not only amongst Asians, but also among besotted, returned Western travellers. They even had a website to cater for far-flung customers and had a mail order arm, too. It would be a mistake to underestimate him.

Mr Bansi clasped his bony hands round his knees, darted a narrowed glance at his wife and told Casey, 'I found Chandra a charming girl.' Beside him the jelly set to wobbling again, but this time she kept silent. He gave them a dry little smile, as much as to say, see, I am master in my own home when it matters, and said, 'Of course, I work long hours and saw little of the girl. She spent her time with my wife and the baby. No doubt she was a little headstrong.' He shrugged. 'But she was a good-looking girl and had been spoilt. Time and more children would have settled her down, persuaded her to give up modern Western notions of what a wife's role should be.'

His eyes moistened. 'Unfortunately, because of racist bigots, she was not given that time. I was pleased to learn that you have two white youths in custody. That is why my wife wonders that you are here, questioning us. Soon they will be charged, yes?'

Casey wondered how they had learned about Gough and

Linklater. But as this was the kind of case where he could expect news to leak, he simply drew a deep breath before advising them that at this stage the white youths were merely possible suspects helping them with their enquiries and had yet to be charged, which was why other aspects of the investigation were continuing. That was why he was now questioning them. Before his courage deserted him, he added that he would need alibis from them, too.

This was greeted with a stunned silence. It didn't last long.

As expected, Mrs Bansi was outraged. 'What for should I provide an alibi? Am I one of these fire-setters the papers write about? Better for you to be charging the real culprits, isn't it, than hounding the bereaved.' She nudged her husband in the side. 'Tell him, Sanjit. What for you sit there while he insults your wife?'

For a moment, Casey thought Sanjit Bansi had finally lost his patience. As a little colour came into the fleshless cheeks his body quivered, in a delicate accompaniment to his wife's more vigorous fortissimo flesh-rippling. But the moment passed. He muttered an aside in rapid Hindi to his wife, then demanded, 'I do not understand why you need alibis from us. And what about these white boys? What for have you not charged them?'

His fluent command of English was deteriorating. Before either of them could fling more questions at him, Casey told them, 'A little matter of evidence, sir. There's also the possibility that they may have alibis.'

'Alibis? What alibis could they have? No doubt alibis supplied by their families.' This from the intemperate Mrs Bansi.

Her more self-controlled husband looked shocked. His cadaverous cheeks seemed to cave in a little more before he rallied. 'But I understood they had made the confessions.'

Casey blinked. This was a leak too far. How had they discovered that? Having felt doubts since the interviews with Gough and Linklater, he hadn't released the news of their custody or confessions to the media. Had Brown-Smith, in spite of his promise to get an extension to their suspects' custody, released it unofficially to one of his many Asian acquaintances in order to pressurize Casey into forgetting his doubts and pressing ahead with the charges? He wouldn't put it past him.

'This I do not understand,' Sanjit Bansi protested. 'This will cause a great agitation in my community. We all feared there would be a whitewash and now we see—'

Casey, well aware of the rising tensions in the Asian community and worried that any demonstrations would bring a violent backlash, was quick to reassure Mr Bansi. 'I promise you, there will be no whitewash. As yet there is insufficient evidence to charge these youths. Someone has been a little premature in releasing the news. We have charged no one. Two white youths have been questioned extensively, but their claims are still being checked out. I hope you will take my word for that and spread it among your community. It will help no one if this case inflames prejudices on either side. Let me assure you that the police service is taking this matter extremely seriously. We have now received the forensic reports on the samples removed from your daughter-in-law's flat. There is little doubt that we are now investigating a double murder.' Casey didn't mention the other possibility – that Gwyn Owen was right and that Chandra had committed sati. Besides, he didn't believe it. He preferred to concentrate on the facts of the case, such as the discarded vacuum flask with its petrol dregs. 'That being so, the investigation into your daughter-in-law's death and that of her baby will not lack resources. Every aspect of her life will be examined for clues to the person or persons responsible. We will find whoever murdered them Mr Bansi, Mrs Bansi, let me assure you of that. And when we do and they are judged guilty in a court of law, they will suffer the full rigour of that law.'

As he watched, Mr and Mrs Bansi exchanged involuntary glances, in which anxiety was writ large. Could they be worried that the digging into Chandra's life would bring revelations even more damaging than their less than kind treatment of Chandra and her daughter?

He paused for several seconds to let them consider their position, before again asking for their whereabouts at the relevant time, adding quickly that it was merely routine before Mrs Bansi could make any further protests. 'Chandra's family will also be asked to supply alibis. I'm sure they will be only too happy to do so if it means we don't waste time and resources that should be used on finding the real culprits.' He hoped they would be, anyway.

Roop Bansi was evidently little mollified on learning this. Obviously, being involved in something as common as a police investigation was little to her taste. Still, she provided the answer to Casey's question.

'I was at home, of course. Where else is it a good wife would be at lunchtime but at home preparing her husband's meal?'

'And that would cover what times exactly?'

Eventually, after much scowling and tutting and mutterings in Hindi, she told him, 'All morning I was here, isn't it? My husband he come in from his work at twenty to one. He leave about twenty, twenty-five to two. I went out on the dot of two do my shopping for the evening meal. Twice a day I buy the fresh food. I am a dutiful wife as my husband will tell you. He is served none of that expensive frozen muck in this house. He is served only the best.'

Casey wondered at the man's thinness if that was the case. Wisely, he kept the thought to himself.

Getting Mr Bansi's alibi was an easier matter, and five minutes later he and Shazia Singh were outside on the pavement wearing matching expressions of relief. As they climbed into the car, Casey asked, 'How would you fancy *her* for a mother-in-law?'

Shazia gave a delicate shudder. 'I wouldn't. Fortunately, my parents are more enlightened, more modern than Chandra's family seem to be. They are quite happy for me to have a career. They have even agreed to let me choose my own husband as long as they can pretend to the community that it was *their* choice. It's all about keeping face, Inspector. The Japanese could learn a thing or two about face from Asians.'

Casey, with his own difficulties about 'face', should the existence of his hippie, drug-taking parents become common knowledge, gave a sympathetic nod.

They got in the car and he asked, 'Did you manage to catch any of those mutterings in Hindi?'

She shook her head. 'No. But I can tell you what Mrs Bansi called her daughter-in-law.'

Shazia Singh must have been a lover of Bollywood films; certainly, she understood the importance of the dramatic moment, as before she made her revelation she busied herself in doing up her seatbelt and adjusting her uniform, rising the tension nicely.

'The Hindi word, *randi*, means 'widow'.'

Casey frowned. 'I don't understand. Why would calling her daughter-in-law a widow shock you? It was what she was, after all.'

'Because of the other meaning it has come to have. Historically, Hindu widows were often forced to have sex with other men in their husbands' families, or to sell sex.' Shazia's delicate features were demure as she explained, 'The practice was once so widespread that the Hindi word for widow – *randi* – has become synonymous with prostitute. That is what she called her daughter-in-law. A prostitute.'

Casey fastened his own seatbelt. Lips pursed in contemplation, he drove slowly back to the station while he considered what he had learned. Had Roop Bansi thought she had reason for calling her daughter-in-law a prostitute? Had Chandra had an affair with Mark Farrell, or some other unsuitable man, and been found out? Farrell had denied there was any romantic attachment between them. Had he lied to them about the kind of relationship he had with Chandra? And if he had successfully pursued the desired affair with Chandra Bansi, had it been before or after she was widowed?

Far from Mrs Bansi protesting that she could not have had anything to do with Chandra's death, it turned out that, as the only alibi each had was supplied by the other, this meant that in reality *neither* of the Bansis had a real alibi for the relevant time. It was only a couple of miles from their house to Chandra's flat. And provided the petrol was ready to hand, it would be a moment's work to splash it in the back room and throw a match to it – and Chandra.

Poor girl. How had she borne living with her uncongenial mother-in-law? With a husband who was overly possessive and who allowed her little privacy? Casey, mostly used to his own space and the freedom to do as he pleased with that space, would have felt suffocated. As it was he was finding sharing his home with his parents a daily endurance test, and stayed out of the house as much as possible. With a constantly crying baby who would only earn her more criticism from her mother-in-law, Chandra must have been truly desperate.

After the initial shock of losing her husband so suddenly and then being thrown out of the house by her in-laws, she must surely have found the peace and freedom of her little flat a paradise in comparison. OK, the baby still cried, but at least her cries were no longer accompanied by constant carping. Loneliness, too, could be borne; how much more lonely would she have been in her unhappy marriage?

Chandra's brother and Mark Farrell had both said she had been depressed. Her younger sister had said she was lonely – yet she admitted she hadn't seen her, so how could she know? Angela Neerey, who *had* seen her, had told him that Chandra had been trying to get her life together. After the early, disastrous marriage, she had wisely refused to attempt a second and had been sensibly considering her future and finding out about college courses. Who knew what she might have made of the rest of her life? What a tragedy that her first tentative steps towards that future had ended so abruptly.

Two young lives, with all the promise that the future might bring, snuffed out in a few tortuous moments. The little paradise of her flat turning into the entrance to another, altogether premature paradise.

Who among his crop of suspects could have done such a thing? It would be easy – too easy – to cling hopefully to their two earliest suspects, Gough and Linklater. And with the information Catt had supplied concerning Gough, though as yet unsubstantiated, Casey had begun to believe the pair had claimed the Chandra Bansi arson out of mindless braggadocio, two deaths being two up on what they had previously achieved. He seriously doubted that either of the two confessions would turn out to be viable. In the hope that he would get firm evidence one way or the other he had put off breaking the news to Superintendent Brown-Smith. But it couldn't be put off much longer. Privileges of rank, indeed.

And as for the Bansis, though Casey thought it unlikely that Mr Bansi alone would be capable of setting a fire – unless it was one under his own wife – he was also without an alibi. Besides, who knew what his wife might goad him to do? And after what Shazia had told him about Mrs Bansi's name-calling of Chandra, he felt justified in adding them both to the growing array of potential suspects.

It was turning into quite a list. Casey was beginning to feel seriously bogged down by the size of it. He decided he needed some time away from the investigation if he wasn't to become snowed under with the ever-growing possibilities. He had yet to make time to speak to Tara Tompkins, Wayne Gough's girlfriend. The vicar she had claimed as her witness was still away and it seemed the case was going nowhere. His daily sessions with Superintendent Brown-Smith were becoming more heated; despite agreeing to extend the detention while further enquiries were made, the super was champing at the bit to get the pair charged. Of course, he was under pressure himself. Racist attacks had become something of a political football and this was one that the entire team wanted a kick at.

He hadn't even found time yet to start sorting out his parents' debts. They would still be living with him by the time Rachel returned from her extended tour at this rate.

So, when they got back to the station, even before he went in search of Catt to whisk him off to The Lamb, he got in touch with his bank. To his surprise he was told a limit had been put on loans for the current month. He was advised to get the credit on his card extended instead. Saying he'd think about it, Casey replaced the receiver. Extend his credit limit indeed – at the interest they charged? He really must get around to investigating one of the new, lower interest-charging credit cards, he decided. But it was one thing to pay off their debts. What he really needed to do was try to ensure they didn't get into debt again. They didn't have a bank account as they had been too irresponsible too often in the past, which made them a bad risk, so regular direct debit bill payment was out. But he remembered reading that some banks now offered accounts for the more impecunious and financially irresponsible customer. They didn't provide overdraft facilities or cheque books, but they did allow the setting up of direct debits and supplied a debit card. That sort of account might be the answer. The difficult bit would be getting his parents to supply all the proof of identity that banks nowadays demanded.

He had taken a cutting of the article, but unfortunately his careful hoarding had been to no avail. Since his parents' arrival the cutting had vanished from its place of safe keeping. He half suspected one of his parents of deliberately removing it so they could continue their comfortable, free sojourn at his house.

Shaking his head at his own undutiful suspicions, he decided he'd do a bit of ringing around after lunch and try to find out who offered such an account. He could worry about the paperwork when he had the relevant information to hand. His stomach rumbled and he went to find Catt to persuade him to accompany him to The Lamb. They needed some lunch, anyway.

The saloon bar was full, but they managed to find an empty table in the corner. Once they were settled with plates of fragrant chicken curry in front of them, Casey told Catt of the interview with Chandra's in-laws.

'Formidable woman,' said Casey as he began to eat. 'It's obvious who wears the *dhotis* in that house.'

Catt emptied half of his pint of Adnam's bitter. 'I thought Asian men were firmly head of the household. Last bastion of male chauvinism and all that.'

'Not in this case. She didn't even pretend to wifely submission, apart from when she realized her tongue was running away with her. Funny when you think of it, considering she thought Chandra too westernized, too opinionated.'

'Case of them being too alike, perhaps? So what next?' Catt asked. 'If, as you suspect, he's going to be disappointed over Gough and Linklater, Brownjob's going to want to hear that we're making progress in another direction.'

Casey was well aware of it. It was something the superintendent had become increasingly emphatic about. He wanted somebody, anybody – anybody *white*, anyway – charged in this case before it damaged his career. Hence the leaks.

'No more convenient white, racist arsonists appeared on the horizon?' Catt asked.

'None that I've come across.' Casey suddenly lost his appetite and he thrust his half-finished meal away. He didn't mention to Catt his suspicions that Brown-Smith had been leaking to the Asian community. Catt could be impulsive and had already faced one disciplinary board about his 'attitude'. Casey was anxious that he didn't face another one.

Perhaps it had been both selfish and unwise of him to insist on Catt assisting him on this case. Although he had kept an admirable low profile, Casey often caught waves of simmering resentment emanating from his sergeant. He couldn't altogether blame him. He just hoped this case was concluded before Catt forgot his vow of silence.

'Someone must have seen something,' Casey said quietly. 'So far, we've only questioned Chandra's neighbours. Maybe we ought to extend the house-to-house to the neighbours of the Bansis, given Mrs Bansi's vindictive attitude to her daughter-in-law. Maybe, if we find evidence that they're lying, we might be able to move the case forward. Maybe the vociferous Mrs Bansi was going in for a double bluff, thinking that her very outspokenness against Chandra would stop us suspecting her.'

Catt nodded. 'Could be. If one of the Bansi's neighbours saw either of them around the vicinity of Chandra's flat at the relevant time we might begin to get some sort of lever. All we need is a shred of proof that they're lying and we can get them in for some serious questioning.'

'Hold on,' said Casey. 'I told you what Brown-Smith demanded. Kid gloves, ThomCatt, kid gloves.'

'I know,' Catt said, his expression suddenly surly. 'But at least I can get the house-to-house organized. I'll do it this afternoon.' A person of mercurial, ever-changing moods, Catt's surly expression was now replaced by pursed lips and a teasing glance. 'Don't worry. I must be getting as politically correct as Brian Brownjob, because I'll be praying we find nothing.'

Casey raised his eyebrows at this.

'All right,' Catt conceded. 'Perhaps I've a way to go on the PC front. Let's just say I don't fancy tackling the human blancmange. She doesn't sound so sweet to me.'

Casey muttered an 'Ah' of comprehension at this. 'Had me worried for a moment,' he said softly. 'Thought you'd had a conversion. And you know what they say about converts.'

Eleven

Tara Tompkins had vanished. When Casey went round to the flat she shared with two other girls in the town, he was told that she had gone away. When he asked if they knew where, they denied it. Convinced that this news would prompt the superintendent to insist on going ahead with charging Gough and Linklater, Casey pressed them with more questions.

Eventually, one of them admitted that Tara had left a note.

'Where is it? Please let me see it.'

'It won't tell you anything,' Amanda, the tall redhead told him pertly. 'All it says is that she's going away. Nothing about where or for how long. So you know as much as we do.'

Casey was in no mood to be gainsaid. 'Please, just give me the note.'

With a flounce, Amanda turned and picked up her shoulder bag. 'Here.' She thrust a single sheet of paper at him. 'I told you you'd be none the wiser. And before you ask, no, she didn't tell us any more. We didn't even see her. She was gone when I got back from college. Better for her if she stays away. That oaf, Wayne, will go down for sure without her. We could never understand what she saw in him anyway.'

'Why do you say that he'll go down for sure without her? *Can* she alibi him?'

'Said she could, but really I've no idea. She didn't confide in us. I suppose we've had one go too many at attempting to make her leave Wayne. She's become very prickly about him. Tara must have a martyr complex to want to take him on.'

Casey was inclined to agree. Disappointed that he had

missed Tara by a few short hours, he headed back to the station. He could only hope that Catt, out digging amongst his assorted snouts, came up with something.

When he got back to the office it was to find out that Catt *had* come up with something. Though whether it was a something the superintendent would want to hear was another matter. Catt had discovered that Rathi Khan was up to his eyes in serious debt to some very unpleasant moneylenders in India.

'Rumour is they've been threatening his family out there. Maybe they were threatening his family *here*, too.'

Casey stared at him. 'Go on.'

'They wanted their money, so would be unlikely to target Rathi Khan himself or his house in case their debtor died. But—'

'But Chandra and her baby would be easy targets?' Casey finished for him.

Catt nodded. 'And targeting them would make the loan sharks' points just as starkly. But even this cloud has a silver lining, because if that turned out to be what happened, it would please Brownjob. No one likes loan sharks of whatever ethnic stamp, not even him. Their torching of the flat would have given Rathi Khan a very heavy warning not to mess with them again *and* made sure he could repay them from the fire insurance. Maybe, to muddy the waters, they even hired white thugs through intermediaries to do the deed.'

Casey asked, 'So how did you find out about these debts of Khan's?'

'Multicultural, me,' Catt said airily. 'My foundling upbringing might not have given many advantages, but one of the children's homes I was in had several Asian kids. A couple of them have remained friends. They even supply me with information occasionally.'

'Asian snouts?' Casey was impressed. In his experience Asians weren't much given to snitching to the police. Certainly not about members of their own community. He had a feeling that Superintendent Brown-Smith wouldn't approve. But, on the principle that what he didn't know would cause him no PC grief, Casey questioned Catt further. 'Are these snouts reliable? I don't want to pursue yet another strand if it turns out they've supplied dud information.'

Catt looked down his nose at this slur. If he'd had a tail he'd have whisked it high and stalked off. 'Best snouts I've ever had. You know how industrious Asians are. Besides, I was brought up with these guys. I think you might find that we brats from the kids' home stick together. What other loyalties did any of us have or have reason to have?'

'Even though you're now a copper?'

'I'm a *foundling* copper. There's a difference.'

Catt had a fondness for the word 'foundling' with all its Dickensian implications of deprivation and abandonment. It was as though he wanted to be sure to mention his background before anyone else could. Casey managed a tight smile at this. For all Catt's ready talk of abandonment, he didn't understand what it was to be truly abandoned at all.

During the months that Casey had spent as a child in India on the hippie trail with his parents, he had been abandoned more times than he could count. On the first occasion, they had been in the country for less than a week. Everything was alien, strange, frightening. He'd been not quite ten.

His mother, spaced out as she had so often been in those days, had told him that she and his father were just going out to see some amazing local holy man they'd heard about and would be gone an hour or two.

Three days later, when they had still not returned, Casey was frantic with worry. Not to mention dizzy from hunger. Eating had never been high in his parents' priorities and the only food in the backpack was about an ounce of rice.

That had been the first of many such abandonments. Gradually, Casey had learned self-sufficiency. After that, wherever his parents' hippie wanderings took them he generally managed to find himself some sort of paying work;

mostly running errands for other hippies or, preferably, for the more wealthy tourists who paid in cash rather than hashish. At least it meant he could feed himself. No, Thom-Catt, with his three-square-meals-a-day children's home fare, didn't grasp the meaning of 'abandonment' at all.

Strangely, Casey's experiences hadn't turned him into the streetwise urchin that he imagined Catt had been as a child. They had made him old for his years and more than a bit of a worrier. And more responsible, mature and self-sufficient than any ten-year-old should ever need to be. It was a time in his life he rarely spoke about, even now.

But now was not the time for such reflections. Not when Catt had begun to reveal something else.

'As I said, I've found my Asian snouts reliable in the past. But, as it happens, I've had the same information supplied by another source.'

Casey's eyebrows cocked. 'Oh?'

'A disgruntled ex-employee of Mr Khan. My Asian snouts put me on to him.' Casey wondered if he should remind Catt that he had been ordered to stay away from Asian witnesses, but decided to let it drop. 'Seems Khan is not only in serious hock to these Asian Shylocks, but one of his other properties had a serious fire last year. Apparently, he made a successful insurance claim and got the loan sharks off his back then. I've got on to the insurance firm and the information checks out.'

'And you think, like our other arsonists, Gough and Linklater, that he might be starting to make a habit of it?'

Catt shrugged. 'Wouldn't be the first time. Insurance companies are regarded as fair game by most people.'

'But his daughter and granddaughter were in the house,' Casey protested.

'Which brings us back to the loan sharks being the arsonists.'

Casey sat back. They had come full circle. 'Very well. I'm going to pay another visit to Mr Khan. Find Shazia Singh, will you? I'd like her to accompany me. In view of this new information I want to check he *was* at the High Street shop last Saturday when Chandra's fire was set. While I'm doing that, I want you to get back to your snouts and find out if they know anything more. And try that vicar again. If Gough at least is out of it as far as Chandra's case goes, the sooner we get it confirmed the better.'

The same racks of clothes still stood outside Rathi Khan's High Street shop, cluttering the pavement, still full of low-priced dresses and trousers. Funny, but Casey felt that in the interval since their last visit so much had happened that the entire stock should have changed.

The weather was still warm, only now it was becoming oppressive. The shop door was open to let in some air and from the open doorway came the sound of Indian music, the 'wailing' kind, as Dean Linklater would no doubt describe it. Casey stopped to listen. After a minute he asked Shazia what the song was about.

'What Hindi songs are always about,' she told him with an amused glance from her bold tawny eyes. 'Thrills and spills, love and passion, with a hero who is good to his mum and who always marries a virgin. The usual Bollywood stuff. "Masala movies" they're called, because like a good curry there is a little bit of every flavour in one dish. Maybe you ought to try going to see an Indian film, sir,' she suggested artlessly. 'It would give you a glimpse beneath the surface of Indian life, if nothing else.'

The suggestion had been made in that half-teasing, half-challenging way he had come to recognize. He wondered if she thought him too stuffy and conservative to take her up on her suggestion. He felt sufficiently challenged to mutter, 'Maybe I will.' There was a cinema just around the corner that showed mostly Indian films. A visit might provide him with an 'in' on an aspect of Indian culture and give him a different perspective from the usual runaway bride scenario, which was all that hit the headlines here. Perhaps he could ask his mother to go with him. She had spent a lot of time at the cinema whilst they were in India – when she wasn't haggling at the bazaars or disappearing to spend time with fake fakirs.

He'd forgotten what a jolt to the senses the shop's interior was. The pastel shades of England outside on the street seemed wishy-washy when contrasted with the vivid colours of the subcontinent. Like spatterings from an artist's palette, brilliant bales of material – a deep, rich emerald, a blue as deep as Indian summer skies, a wanton's red, lustrous golden saffron – were stacked where they could fit. Pinned to the walls were the *cholis* or tight-fitting bodices worn under saris, as well as a wide selection of *jootis*, the traditional Indian shoes with their exquisite, colourful embroidery and curled toes that his mother still favoured. He'd prevailed on her to only wear them about the house.

Some of the *chotis* and saris were very ornate, with extensive gold metal embroidery. They looked expensive even to Casey's untutored eye.

There was no sign of Rathi Khan at the shop today. Casey decided to stay anyway and question Mrs Ghosh. Govind Ghosh, the sole assistant, was busy with half a dozen Asian women of varying ages who all seemed to be together. They gesticulated excitedly, chattering like magpies, as length after length of material was spread out on the sideboard counter and pored over. More chatter ensued as the qualities of each material were discussed, until finally one of the younger women fell upon the latest material displayed. And an even more animated discussion broke out.

Apparently she wasn't to be swayed from her choice. Hugging the gorgeous red, heavily embroided brocade proprietarily to her bosom with one hand, she waved off objections with the other, talking vociferously all the while.

Around the mid-forties, neat-figured and with bright, busy brown eyes that seemed to miss little, Govind Ghosh was evidently an excellent saleswoman, for she immediately bustled about and in a matter of seconds had produced the matching *choli* and an assortment of *jootis* and other finishing touches, and set about completing the sale before the bride could be persuaded to change her mind. Casey hoped she would prove as efficient when it came to answering his questions.

He was beginning to recognize the particular lilt and cadence of Hindi even if he could remember little of the vocabulary. 'Why that one, I wonder?' he murmured now as he nodded his head at the selected material. 'What is it, anyway?' he asked, nodding as the girl's choice of sari was folded and wrapped. 'Some sort of fancy party outfit?'

Shazia Singh smiled. 'In a way. It's wedding sari. Red for a bride. Unlike the Western tradition, white is for widows, not brides.'

Casey nodded. He recalled Shazia telling him that before; he wondered he hadn't remembered it from his travels, but then weddings and their requisite accoutrements were not at the top of most ten-year-old boys' lists of things to know. He'd spent most of his time in India making sure he had a bed for the night and finding work so he could buy food. 'Strange how such different customs evolve.'

The bride-to-be went off clutching her purchases, followed by her small army of advisors, and the assistant turned to Casey and Shazia Singh with a smile. She clearly remembered them from their previous visit for she apologized for keeping them waiting, then asked, 'How is Mr Khan? Such a dreadful business.'

Casey nodded. 'He seems to be bearing up, Mrs Ghosh. He hasn't been in today?'

'No. With what has happened, I wouldn't expect him. Normally, he's always here on a Wednesday and Saturday, checking the stock and so on.' Mrs Ghosh shook her head worriedly. 'It still hasn't been done from last Saturday. Mr Khan went rushing off at lunchtime that day and I haven't seen him since.'

Casey's ears pricked up. 'He went rushing off, you say? What time was this?'

'About one thirty it would have been. After he had the

phone call. Poor man to get such distressing news, and on Krishna's birthday, too – a day that should bring only auspicious happenings, not tragedy.'

Casey frowned. As far as he was aware no one but Catt had rung the shop last Saturday, the day of Chandra's death, and Catt had only rung to check that Rathi Khan *was* there, not to break the bad news. So who had? Maybe Chandra's next-door neighbour had called him? But as Casey recalled that Angela Neerey had been unsure if the High Street shop was one of Mr Khan's, he realized it was unlikely. It was curious. So was the timing of the phone call. He questioned Mrs Ghosh further, but it turned out that she had only assumed the call and the fire were connected afterwards, as Rathi Khan apparently hadn't uttered a word of explanation before he left the shop.

'How long was Mr Khan here, before he rushed off?' Casey asked.

'He'd only arrived five minutes before. Said he'd had trouble with his car. I teased him that it was time he bought a new one. Always he has the new cars, but I suppose with his parents over from home he hasn't had time to arrange a new one.'

By Casey's estimation Mr Khan had had three years in which to make such a purchase. He could only presume that Govind Ghosh knew little about cars and less about her boss's financial situation.

It was interesting that Khan hadn't arrived at the shop till around 1.25 p.m. He could have been anywhere. It meant he was still under suspicion, especially after what ThomCatt had discovered.

What the assistant said next stunned him, pointing as it did to Khan's possible involvement in the deaths, however accidentally. 'Such a dreadful business. And so desperately sad that the fire happened on a day Chandra and the baby weren't even suppose to be there.'

Casey frowned, glanced at Shazia Singh and said, 'What do you mean?'

'Chandra was meant to be in London that day, her and the baby. Visiting cousins, I think. It was all arranged.'

Casey's frown deepened. 'Are you saying that Mr Khan, too, assumed his daughter and granddaughter would be in London that day?'

'Well yes. Of course. He was the one who arranged the trip. He was worried about her and thought it would cheer her up. It was only later that he realized she hadn't gone. But surely Mr Khan told you all this when you spoke to him?'

'No. He must have forgotten in all the upset,' was Casey's oblique comment as Govind Ghosh looked doubtfully at him. Brought up by hippie parents in a loving but disorganized and permanently changing home as they kept one step ahead of bailiffs, Casey found it more difficult than the cynical ThomCatt to believe Chandra's father could have been responsible for her murder and that of her baby. Catt's abandonment as a toddler had left him badly scarred emotionally under his cocky, protective shell. He couldn't be expected to have much faith in parental love. Casey admitted he had little reason to have much faith in it either, but he thought most parents would draw the line at killing their own offspring. Now he asked, 'So when did he realize she hadn't gone, that she was in fact still at the flat?'

Mrs Ghosh hesitated then, with a fatalistic shrug she ploughed on anyway, in the manner of one whose indiscretions have gone too far for backtracking. 'It was the telephone call that made him realize they hadn't gone to London. At least, I can only assume it must have been that as I have never seen him so upset. I don't know who the call was from but immediately after, without a word to me, he rushed out. He didn't even stop to get his jacket, which was most unlike him. Mr Khan is a very particular gentleman always. Never goes anywhere without his jacket and his tie all nicely done up like so, never mind what the weather is doing. As I said, I've never seen him in such a state.'

'And you say you have no idea who the phone call was from?'

Mrs Ghosh shook her head again. 'No. And Mr Khan didn't say. Just pushed past me as if I wasn't there. Most unlike him to be so rude. He was usually a very well-mannered, considerate gentleman.'

That Rathi Khan had expected his daughter and grand-daughter to be away from the flat on the day of the fire certainly strengthened their suspicions that he might have had something to do with it, or at least arranged for a couple of thugs to torch the place for the insurance in their presumed absence. If so, what must he be feeling now?

When Casey got back to the station he told Catt what he'd learned. 'It's got to be connected to the fire. Timewise, it's too much of a coincidence to be anything else.'

Catt nodded. 'Perhaps one of Chandra's neighbours phoned him?'

'Possibly, though unlikely. But get the house-to-house team to check it out. Get on to British Telecom, too. I want to know who made the call. Then I think we'll go and have a word with Mr Khan and see what he can add.'

None of Chandra's neighbours admitted ringing her father. But as Chandra had only lived at the flat for a few weeks it was unlikely, as Casey had said, that most of them would even know her by sight, never mind have reached the stage of intimacy that would induce the exchange of contact numbers. So who had made the telephone call? It was a bit of a mystery and one that Casey wanted cleared up as soon as possible. All that British Telecom had been able to tell them was that it had been made from a public phone box a few streets away from both the Khan and Bansi homes. Their only hope of an answer lay in asking the call's recipient. Even if he chose to lie to them about it, for whatever reason, such an evasion would be almost as revealing as the truth.

Twelve

There was no answer at Rathi Khan's home, though Casey could have sworn he caught a brief glimpse of a face at the front window. But further knocking produced no response. They had just got back into the car when Mr Khan's Rover pulled into the drive.

They got out of the car again and approached as he locked his car door. He seemed to be making a bit of a production over it.

He turned slowly to face them. 'Inspector.' He nodded at Catt. He looked tense, expectant, as if he was gearing himself up for more bad news. 'Has anything happened?' he asked quickly. 'Have you found—'

'Nothing yet,' Casey told him. 'There are just one or two things that we'd like to clear up. Perhaps we can come in?'

'Of course. Of course. *Kshama* – sorry my wife didn't let you in,' he threw over his shoulder, 'but since Chandra's tragedy I have forbidden her to open the door unless me or my son are in the house.'

'Very sensible.' Was that an indication that Rathi Khan believed the loan sharks might have been responsible for the arson attack? Casey wondered. Or was it simply to plant the possibility in Casey's mind in case he had already found out about Mr Khan's debts?

As before, Rathi Khan led them into the double-aspect living room. It was empty today.

'Please to sit down.' Rathi Khan gestured to one of the large yellow settees. 'Would you like some tea? Coffee?'

'Nothing, thank you. This should be just a brief visit.' Was it his imagination or had a fleeting look of relief crossed Rathi Khan's face?

'How can I help you?' Like a guest uncertain of his welcome, Mr Khan perched on the edge of one of his armchairs and gazed anxiously at them. He had lost weight since the tragedy. And although still dressed 'just so' as Mrs Ghosh had described, his suit hung off him. He looked ill.

'It's really just routine stuff.' Casey's tone was reassuring. 'Just a matter of getting things out of the way so we can concentrate on more important aspects of the crime. All we wanted to do was check with yourself and your family who was where, and at what times, on the day your daughter and her baby died. We—'

'You ask us? Her family?' Although Rathi Khan sounded shocked to be asked such a question, a look of wariness clouded his eyes. He stared at them, his expression tense. 'But what can you possibly want to know that for?' He gazed anxiously from Casey to the silent Catt and back again. 'This I do not understand.'

Casey sat back and forced himself to relax. His body language needed to be as convincing as his arguments if he was to persuade Rathi Khan that it really *was* just routine. Otherwise, he might get on the phone to the station and Superintendent Brown-Smith was prone to come down hard and heavy on those whose names featured in an official complaint from one of the ethnic minorities.

'As I said, it's simply routine. It has to be done, but it's just for the books, really. I should have asked you before of course, but after such a tragedy I couldn't quite find the words. But once we get such straightforward matters out of the way we can concentrate on more important aspects.'

Was Mr Khan taken in by his Judas words? he wondered. Probably not. He was an intelligent man. Intelligent enough, Casey hoped, to understand that he would keep probing till he got some answers. He must realize that the victims' family would be on their list of suspects. So many murders were domestics of one sort or another that even Superintendent Brown-Smith had to accept that possibility here. Rathi Khan, too, appeared to recognize this as his protestations seemed more perfunctory than genuine.

Casey made a show of consulting his notes. 'For instance, we know you were in your High Street shop on Saturday August thirty-first and arrived there about one twenty-five p.m. But then you received a phone call and rushed out again. Perhaps you could tell us who called you and where you went?'

They had arrived at the shop shortly after two and he had been there then. So where had he gone and what had he done in the previous half-hour that was so pressing?

Rathi Khan appeared puzzled. 'Phone call? What phone call is this that you speak of? I remember no phone call.'

'Perhaps I can refresh your memory? Your assistant, Mrs Ghosh, was quite clear. She told us you rushed off without your jacket – not your normal habit, I gather? It must have been something urgent. She told us the call had visibly upset you.'

An expression of concentrated thought furrowed Mr Khan's high forehead, then his expression cleared. 'Of course. How foolish of me. But with all this tragic business I had clean forgotten. My son rang me to tell me my wife had had an accident in the kitchen. She burned her hands when a pan of hot ghee went up. Really, he made it sound quite horrific. Naturally, I was upset.'

'I see.' Strange then, thought Casey, that with a phone in the house and a mobile in his pocket, Dan Khan had found it necessary to leave the family home and make the call from a public phonebox.

Casey decided not to question Mr Khan about it for the time being. 'Tread warily, with kid gloves,' had been Superintendent Brown-Smith's injunction. And as far as he could, Casey intended to continue to abide by it and the restrictions it imposed.

'Yet, obviously your wife's injuries weren't as serious as you feared.' Casey certainly hadn't noticed any burns on Mrs Khan's hands or face on the day of the arson; certainly no marks that would have warranted calling her husband from his work.

'It was a big fuss over nothing. Which is why I returned to work almost straight away. Women, they are the most dreadful drama queens.'

'My mother always says it is the male of the species who are the drama queens. She insists that women are far more stoical. On the whole I have found she's right. Your wife, son, daughter-in-law and parents were at home when you got here?' Mr Khan nodded, then corrected himself. 'No. I forgot. My daughter-in-law was out with my daughter and granddaughter.'

Although he had corrected himself, Rathi Khan hadn't corrected the lie. Because if Dan Khan had made that phone call as his father claimed, he had certainly not made it from here. So where had he been? And, more to the point, what had he been doing?

'It was a normal day, would you say? Until the fire?'

Rathi Khan looked curiously at him as if he couldn't see the point of such a question. He shrugged. 'Yes. My wife rose first to take the tea in bed to my parents, while my daughter-in-law prepared breakfast and got the children up. She took the children out around midday according to my wife, after the household chores were completed. My granddaughter is to start at the local infant school this month and she had to get the child's uniform. My daughter, Kamala, went with them.'

'And before that? Were they all at home all morning?'

'Yes. My wife, of course, has her duties here. She looks after my parents while they are here. She is a good wife and takes her duties seriously. She doesn't work outside the home. As my parents rarely go out, she must remain with them. It would not be the done thing, you understand, to leave them on their own when they are under my roof. My wife and my parents rarely go out unless it is with me or my son in our cars. I'm afraid my parents find England a strange place. I hoped they would settle, but now, after . . . Now I think they want to go home, back to India. My father says they are too old to adapt to new customs. Perhaps he is right.'

Casey might have remarked that he, too, found England a strange place, an alien place, even, from the country he had known as a boy. But, of course, he kept such thoughts to himself. He checked that Devdan, the son, was also at home all that morning. Dan Khan worked for his father, but had apparently had a day off and had spent part of it with his family. Apparently he didn't neglect his plain wife *all* the time.

Casey paused, then asked, 'Tell me, Mr Khan. Was your daughter's marriage happy?'

A spasm of pure anguish crossed Rathi Khan's aquiline features at the question. But then he rallied. Casey could almost trace the thought processes that led there. Because should he begin to question whether the early marriage he had arranged for his daughter might have led to her untimely and agonising death he wouldn't be able to bear it. And the best way to avoid such painful introspection lay in strenuous denial. 'Of course it was happy. My Chandra was adored by her husband.'

This was delicate ground. Casey could almost feel Superintendent Brown-Smith perched on his shoulder, anxiously censoring further questions along such lines. But as this was a murder enquiry, Casey felt the weight of the two young victims on his other shoulder and he shrugged the super off, stiffened his spine and continued. 'But I understood theirs was an arranged marriage. That precludes any "of course" as regards personal love or happiness, surely? How long had they known one another?'

'For many years. Since they were children. Always our families have socialized together. Ever since Mr and Mrs Bansi and my wife and I settled here. Mr Bansi is a man of business, like myself. We meet often for that reason, and at the temple, of course. Both our families saw a lot of each other. Chandra was perfectly happy to accept Magan Bansi as her husband.'

That wasn't quite how Chandra's neighbour had told it. And adoration to one person could so easily seem like jealousy and control for the person on the receiving end. Casey had witnessed such behaviour all too often when called out to domestics in his uniformed days. Asian families weren't immune from such situations. Casey, only too aware that not everything about the East was mystical and wonderful, was determined not to be made to feel apologetic for stating the obvious truth. Asians could be quick to criticize Western marriages with their admittedly appalling divorce statistics, while vigorously protesting any criticism, however mild, of their own marital customs which, he knew only too well, concealed much misery behind the walls of the marital home. He suspected that if the Asian womenfolk weren't kept so subjugated they, too, would be clamouring for divorce. Of course, one wasn't supposed to say this.

'And they had both been agreeable to the marriage from the first?'

Mr Khan was halfway through a second 'of course' when he presumably thought better of it and bit the words off. His natural desire to convince Casey – and perhaps himself – how wonderful the match he had made for his daughter had been, was superceded by the need for explanations. 'It was a very good match for Chandra. She knew that, which is why after taking time to consider it she sensibly agreed. Perhaps our two cultures have different ideas about happiness, Inspector. For us, marriage is a social contract, joining two people and their families. It is the couple's duty to make the marriage work. Happiness comes from doing one's duty willingly and well, so as to provide a stable background in which to nurture children. The belief in romantic love as practised in the West is an illusion, as we learn too well from the divorce statistics. Better to start with simple liking and friendship. The rest can grow.'

It was a valid point. But Casey hadn't been challenging the *idea* of arranged marriages as such, merely the suggestion that such marriages were better or happier than the idealized Western love match. However, he didn't pursue the point.

'Why are you asking about her marriage, anyway?' Rathi Khan now asked. 'What has this to do with Chandra's death? What can it possibly have to do with it?'

Casey had been expecting such questions. It had been revealing that his probing hadn't immediately been challenged. 'Probably nothing,' he soothed. Possibly everything, he added silently to himself. 'But every piece of information is of value in finding the truth. The trouble is, at the beginning of an investigation, it's often impossible to recognize what is vital and what is dross. We have no way of knowing at this stage which is which, so we just carry on with the questions, asking anything we can think of.' And in view of Chandra's friendship with Mark Farrell – if that was all it was – and the blame Chandra's in-laws attached to her for their son's death, such questions might turn out to be all too relevant. But he was careful to play this down. It would do no good showing his hand. All it would gain him was another of Superintendent Brown-Smith's interminable lectures.

Rathi Khan still didn't look happy, but he made no more protests. Instead, he asked, 'So, what next, Inspector?'

'We've found those skinheads you said harassed Chandra.' Rathi Khan nodded absently as if he already knew that. Apparently the leak had spread. 'No luck on that front yet, I'm afraid, but investigations are continuing,' Casey told him. 'But if, as I now suspect, that doesn't come to anything, we'll extend our investigation to checking out other well-known local troublemakers and generally widen the scope of the investigation.'

He didn't add that they had already *narrowed* the case. If this turned out to be a domestic, it was essential they thoroughly investigated Chandra's friends and family, in-laws, outlaws, secret lovers – if any. With the added complications of the race element, Casey really didn't want to invite politically correct criticisms, but he had no choice. He just hoped when they finally reached the truth that PC interference didn't end up twisting it beyond recognition.

But after the entire force had been so unfairly branded as institutionally racist, he would be under even greater pressure to find a quick and 'satisfactory' conclusion to the case. Satisfactory to whom had, as yet, not been made clear, though he was sure that given time it would be. But, whatever the pressures brought to bear, Casey was determined that the victims would get justice, however unpalatable in certain quarters the truth of that justice might turn out to be.

He got up to leave and the still splendidly silent Catt followed suit. It was clear they were going to get no more from Rathi Khan today. Mr Khan preceded them along the hallway, but before they reached the entrance, Casey glanced to his left where he noticed a half-open door. It seemed to be given over to a collection of colourful idols. Briefly, he glimpsed Rathi Khan's mother deep in a reverie before the shrine. She was oblivious to the intruder at her door, and with her gazed fixed with fervent intensity on the room's shrine she began a monotonous chanting as, unheeded, tears slipped down her cheeks.

Before Casey could discreetly move on, Rathi Khan appeared beside him and quietly pulled the door shut, commenting, 'Our shrine room. I would appreciate it if you would allow my mother some decent privacy in which to mourn. She has been deeply upset by our tragedy. After my son, Chandra was her favourite grandchild. She and Chandra shared a special closeness.'

Casey nodded. He felt he deserved the rebuke for having intruded on such grief.

Mr Khan opened the front door and ushered them out. He was about to close the door behind them when Casey paused on the threshold, blocking the door. 'I nearly forgot to ask where *you* were that morning, Mr Khan. Perhaps you took your car to the garage? Mrs Ghosh said it was giving you some trouble.'

Mr Khan frowned at this, as though he thought his assistant had been altogether too chatty. 'It was nothing much. Just a loose battery connection. My son had it fixed in a jiffy.' With great dignity, Rathi Khan met Casey's gaze and quietly told him, 'I was at my office all that morning, Inspector, as usual. You can check if you wish. My main office is above my shop in Great Langley.'

Gathering the rest of his still impressive dignity about his now slender frame, Rathi Khan asked simply, 'Now that you are satisfied that myself and my family are, like Chandra and Leela, innocent victims in this tragedy, you will be setting yourself to catching whoever did this thing?'

Casey's reply was equally simple. 'Yes, Mr Khan. Of course. We won't rest until we find whoever committed this evil act. Let me assure you of that.'

Rathi Khan nodded, said, 'That is what I expected,' and shut the door softly behind them.

Catt grimaced as they walked to their car. Released from the Brown-Smith imposed vow of silence, he complained, 'Just our luck to get this case. Whatever we do we're going to be in the wrong.'

They climbed into the car. Casey glanced at him and rebuked mildly, 'Just as well to recognize the fact and deal with it.'

'Wish I could feel confident that the brass would give us decent support. *Any* support. I just wish I didn't have the feeling we're being set up for a fall.'

It was a wish Casey could echo. But becoming paranoid would achieve nothing.

Obviously irritated by Casey's lack of response, Catt quirked an eyebrow at him. 'So, do you think the super's got an ulterior motive for landing us with this case?'

'Time will tell,' was all that Casey said. But like the cynical ThomCatt, he too believed the super had his own agenda. And offering his sturdy support if – when – things got sticky was unlikely to feature too strongly. As Catt had said, for them it was a no-win situation. In the middle, between the racists, racecard players, the force top brass and a pontificating media, he was already being criticized from all sides while he tried to do his job. Ever since Macpherson's inquiry into the murder of black teenager Stephen Lawrence had determined that the British police were 'institutionally racist', a case like this had become a minefield. But, yet again he forced thoughts of these unfairnesses to the back of his mind, aware that if he let such worries affect him too deeply then Chandra and her little daughter might lose any chance they had of receiving justice.

Thirteen

Catt reminded him that he wanted another chat with Angela Neerey about Mark Farrell. 'You don't want to give the super the chance to accuse you of neglecting one of his preferred suspects in order to harass Rathi Khan.'

Casey had been wool-gathering. Absently he said, 'Preferred suspects?'

'White ones. I reckon Brownjob would happily extend Macpherson's remark to include the entire indigenous population as being *constitutionally* racist.'

Casey glanced at him. 'Tom, if you don't tone down your resentment you'll find yourself in front of another disciplinary board.'

'Maybe I should get out of the force altogether,' Catt muttered. 'Let's face it, they don't want honest-to-God coppers like you and me any more. It's so much easier to make criminals out of those we catch – like motorists – than go after the real villains. All the brass want is pen-pushers who can spout the right gobbledegook and spin to the media, and accountants who can fix the arithmetic so the crime figures look good.'

Casey sighed. 'I don't think things have quite come to that pass yet.' But Catt was right about one thing; he *had* neglected this aspect of the investigation and, after ringing Angela Neerey on his mobile to check she was at home, he instructed Catt to head for Ainsley Terrace.

'Mark Farrell?' Angela Neery wiped her little boy's sticky face after his lunch and put him to play on the kitchen floor.

He seemed a cheerful child and beamed toothily at the two policemen. But then, Casey remembered Angela Neerey had said that she, unlike Chandra, had been lucky to have a contented baby. Happy to play by himself, his chatter and laughter as he built his building blocks up only to knock them down again made a warmly domestic background noise to their conversation.

'Yes, I knew him. He came round to Chandra's flat a couple of times when I was there. An intense young man, I thought. Seemed to have a high opinion of himself.'

'Did Chandra say whether they were anything more than friends?' Catt interjected. Frustrated by the vow of silence imposed on him from on high, Catt was evidently determined to question *someone*. Casey, conscious of his sergeant's need to get rid of some of his frustration, was happy to let him get on with it. Catt was fortunate that the witness should come in the attractive form of Angela Neerey.

'Lovers, you mean?' Angela picked up her steaming mug of tea and blew on it while she considered. 'I wouldn't think so. Chandra always said she had had her fill of men. I said to her once that Mark seemed smitten and she just laughed, rather bitterly, I thought, and said he reminded her too much of her late husband. Anyway, her family would kill her, she said, if she took up with a white boy, and life was grim enough for her already, without even more complications.'

Catt nodded. 'What about Farrell? How did he take her rejection?'

Mrs Neerey shrugged. 'Chandra never said, but as he still came round and was perfectly friendly, I imagine he accepted it well enough.'

On the surface, maybe, was Casey's immediate thought as he recalled the sullen expression Farrell had worn when he had spoken of Chandra's rejection. It seemed to be a thought that Catt shared, for now he asked Angela Neerey about it.

'Even when he found out that Chandra's father was trying to arrange another marriage for her?'

'Was he?' She frowned. 'As to that, I've no idea. It's the first I've heard of it. Chandra never mentioned such a possibility.' She gave a shrewd glance at the silent Casey over the rim of her mug. 'I suppose you're wondering how Mark Farrell took the news?'

Casey nodded.

'I wish I could help you, but I've no idea. But as Chandra had already made clear to him that she wanted only friendship, he had no reason to take it badly. No mention was ever made of it between them while I was there.'

Casey had been hoping that, in spite of his doubts, Gough and Linklater's confessions would check out and bring a speedy conclusion to the case, so he hadn't investigated Farrell's alibi. But now that hope was receding. The information Mrs Neerey had supplied was ambiguous. Just because Farrell had appeared to accept didn't make that acceptance a reality. Maybe it was time to see if his alibi held up. Checking his story would be a time-consuming business as he had been on the Continent, travelling round all over the place. But with Superintendent Brown-Smith, the ethnic community and the media all demanding a speedy solution, he couldn't afford to waste any more time.

Angela Neery changed the subject. 'I suppose it'll be months before we have a new neighbour at 5a.' She gave an oblique nod in the direction of Chandra's blackened flat.

Casey, aware of Rathi Khan's money troubles, thought it only too likely. And as Catt seemed to have run out of questions, Casey answered her. 'Pretty unpleasant, I imagine, living so close to a burnt-out ruin.'

'Yes. Especially when I think about poor Chandra and the baby dying in there. It's a constant reminder. If only I'd noticed the fire earlier, they might have been saved.'

'I doubt it.' Casey attempted to console her. 'The petrol meant it took hold quickly. I doubt if anyone could have saved them.'

She gave him a brief smile as if she appreciated his words of consolation. 'I gather it's a complete wreck in there.'

Casey nodded and added, 'Fire's a funny thing. That idol that Chandra had in the corner almost completely escaped the damage.'

'Idol?' She looked puzzled.

'You don't remember it? A blue Krishna figure, about so high.' He measured eighteen inches with his hands.

'Can't say I ever noticed it. Maybe Chandra brought it in from one of the other rooms. She liked to swap things around.' She smiled. 'You never knew whether you'd be sitting under the window or behind the door from visit to visit. She liked to keep busy. I suppose it took her mind off her troubles. She and Leela tended to live and sleep in the back. She found it quieter. I remember her saying that the front room was her glory hole. Being nosy, I looked in once and it was piled high with stuff. I imagine the idol you spoke of came from there and she just brought it out for a change.'

'Perhaps so. Can you remember when it was that you looked in that room?'

Angela Neerey gave him a puzzled glance, but she answered readily enough. 'It was the day before the fire. The Friday. Why do you ask?'

Casey shrugged. 'No particular reason, unless it's desperation to find some answers.' Angela Neerey's reference to the front room of Chandra's flat being piled high with stuff made him question Rathi Khan's possible involvement in an insurance fiddle. Surely, if he had arranged such a thing he would have ensured his daughter's belongings – or most of them at least – were removed? Unless, of course, he had learned from the previous fire at another of his premises that fire-damaged contents were finely raked through by fire investigators who were trained to identify what wasn't still *in situ*.

They hadn't learned anything that put them any further forward and time, like Superintendent Brown-Smith, was pressing. They still had much to do. He glanced at his watch. 'We must be going.' He was anxious to learn if the absent vicar that Gough's girlfriend had mentioned had returned to his flock and wanted Catt to chase it up again. It was surely beyond time that he provided Brown-Smith with some firm leads, even if he had yet to find firm answers.

He drained his mug and put it down on the kitchen table. 'Thanks for the tea and the chat.'

Angela Neerey pulled a face and whisked her little boy off the floor where he had been about to help himself to the cat's lunch. 'I wasn't much help.'

'Oh, I wouldn't say that,' Casey replied. 'Besides,' he smiled his rare smile, 'coming to see you has given me a chance to get out of the office for a while.' And away from the intrusion of the media, who used every ruse to get put through to him.

She laughed. And as the once again silent Catt looked on in amusement, she gave Casey's tall, rangy figure a discreet once-over and told him, 'You know where to find me if ever you feel the need to escape again.'

'That vicar's still errant,' Catt told Casey when he returned to the office much later that afternoon. 'His wife finally admitted she'd forgotten to mention that we needed to speak to him when he rang her. But I've got one piece of news for you, anyway. Dean Linklater's out of it.' Catt took the comb out of his top pocket and ran it through his windblown hair. Like a tabby cat's, it was several shades of tawny, and like a cat, he was always preening it. Casey swore his sergeant was unaware he even did it, or how often.

Catt put his comb away, and perched on the edge of Casey's desk. 'Turns out he was at a job interview at the time the fire at Chandra's flat was set. A letter was delivered for him this morning. His mother opened it. I've just been round to see her again. She insisted Seargent Allen contact me while I was out on the trail of the vicar. Apparently, little Dean hadn't told her about the interview. "Wait till I see him," were her final words before she slammed the door behind me.'

'Idiotic youth. I've a good mind to charge him with wasting police time,' said Casey. 'He's definitely out of it?'

Catt nodded his sleek head with its freshly restored style. 'I spoke to the personnel officer at DIY Warehouse. Dean was there for around two hours, from eleven thirty to one thirty in the afternoon.'

Casey's eyebrows rose. 'Why so long?'

'He had to take tests as well as attend the interview. Seems employers these days have little faith in the education system or their certificates. The personnel officer would have maundered on forever if I'd let him, about the appalling standards of literacy and numeracy in their job applicants. You should have heard him when he got on to the subject of arithmetic. Seems he's had half a rainforest of wood wasted because their skills with a steel measure are on a par with their English.'

Catt rose, insinuated himself with a feline grace into the visitor's chair and added, 'Poor man's older and wiser, so now he tests them before he takes them on.'

With a sudden weariness, Casey lowered himself into his own chair. 'And did Dean get the job?'

'No.'

'Pity. Honest employment might help get him out from under Wayne Gough's malign influence.' Casey shook his head. 'The boy's an all round loser. Tries to be Mr Macho and fails. Tries to be conformist and fails at that as well. Caught between his forceful friend and his forceful mother, I suppose, and tries to please whichever one he spoke to last. Get rid of him with a suitable flea in his ear,' said Casey as, having remembered he had another appointment, he stood up again. 'We'll bail him on the other arson cases. I want you to check on Mark Farrell while I'm out. See if he has any history of violence towards women.'

'You're going out? But . . .' As his mouth turned down, Catt gestured silently at the latest pile of reports awaiting their attention.

'Sorry, ThomCatt, but you'll have to make a start on them on your own,' Casey told him. 'I've got an even more pressing assignment. Another local community meeting.'

'Ah.' Catt pulled a face. 'Your regular mea culpa bit to the Asian community, I suppose?'

'Something like that.'

Catt shook his head. 'Sooner you than me. Macpherson and his wretched report have a lot to answer for. How we're supposed to find the killers of that poor girl and her baby beats me, when I'm forbidden to even speak to any of the Asians involved, and the ones you speak to supply only half answers while their community leaders waste precious time lecturing you – time that could be spent on catching the killers. Wait till you tell them we've had to let Dean Linklater go.'

Two hours later Casey was back. He looked tense, his shoulders hunched under his ears. He'd even bought a packet of cigarettes, though he rarely smoked.

Catt raised his gaze from the mass of reports he had been studying and eyed the cigarettes. 'That bad, huh?'

Casey nodded and slumped in his chair. Naturally enough, on learning that Linklater wasn't to be charged with the killings, the local Asian community hadn't taken the news well. There had been a sudden angry surge towards the platform, and for a little while things had turned ugly. And while the Asian community had stopped short at lynching him and Brown-Smith, he wasn't so sure they would do the same when it came to Linklater. Their anger had been so intense that it needed an outlet. It wouldn't take much for them to take the law into their own hands, search out Linklater and lynch *him*.

Fortunately, between them, he and Brown-Smith had been able to convince them that Linklater really hadn't been responsible for the fatal arson. Of course the hotheads had done their best to increase the already bubbling tensions by shouting, 'No, but he did the others, or are you going to deny that as well?' and almost set the rest off again. He didn't know how long the more restrained leaders would be able to keep them in check.

149

'Have you released Linklater yet?' he now asked Catt.

'No. Thought I'd let him stew for a bit. Let him get in a bit of practise at studying four walls. Why?'

'Just as well. I think we ought to keep him locked up. The mood the local Asians are in I wouldn't like to guarantee his safety on the streets.' Casey closed his eyes and pinched the bridge of his nose. He had a splitting headache. His entire body ached from all the pushing and shoving as well as a few well-aimed punches.

Briefly, he was filled with a longing for the relaxed lifestyle of his parents. Why couldn't he have taken after them and been happy throwing weirdly shaped pots with a bit of leisurely cannabis-growing on the side? On days like today he began to understand the appeal of such a life. The trouble was they had given him little to rebel against, so instead, he'd rebelled by becoming conformist, even going so far as to join the police. Parents, he thought. They really could be the very devil. ThomCatt didn't appreciate his luck in avoiding the complications they brought.

Casey opened his eyes, reached in his drawer for some painkillers and nodded at the pile of reports. 'Anything of interest in that lot?'

'Not so far.' Catt paused before he added, 'I've set the ball rolling to get Mark Farrell's alibi checked out. And while the reports have thrown up nothing to interest you, the phone call I received earlier might. It was about Farrell. I checked on him as you asked, and there was nothing on record with regard to violence to women. Neither was there anything reported according to Sergeant Allen, who should know as he's been here since before Farrell was born. But—'

'But?' Casey echoed, wishing Catt would get on with it.

'Earlier I rang the last school he attended. The same head teacher's still there. It was him that rang me back. Seems Farrell was a bit of a fire-setter in his youth. They managed to hush it up and Farrell promised to be a good boy in future. The head was on a bit of a guilt trip. Seemed desperate for me to reassure him that Farrell had nothing to do with the Bansi deaths.'

'Interesting.' Casey stroked his jaw. He needed another shave. Like his father, he had thick black hair. His father didn't bother to shave, of course. Far too much trouble. Casey had to shave twice, sometimes three times a day. 'And you think he might have resumed his youthful hobby? Consigned her to the flames on the principle that if he couldn't have her, neither would anyone else?'

Catt shrugged. 'It's a possibility. Especially if our lovelorn swain and Chandra exchanged more than the few kisses he claimed before she rejected him again.'

'Angela Neerey didn't think so,' Casey pointed out.

'True. But if Farrell and Chandra were having a fling, I imagine Chandra would have been careful to be discreet. She would have got any unsuitable visitors to come up the back alley rather than the street. She wouldn't want to risk her family finding out. And let's face it, she was in just the sort of emotional turmoil to make her lower her guard. If she did allow Farrell more than kisses and it got back to the family, who knows how they would react?'

'We both know the answer to that one,' Casey replied. There had been enough cases in the national press of young Asian women killed by their families for secretly dating white boys – or even unapproved Asian boys – for them to know only too well. 'Still, I'd be surprised if that was the case here. I think Angela Neerey would have picked up on it. She doesn't seem to miss much.'

'So I noticed. She certainly gave you a thorough once-over.' Catt grinned.

Casey smiled briefly. 'I want you to go and see the head teacher you spoke to. It was Chandra's school as well as Farrell's. Find out who her other friends were. We should have done this before. We would have, but for Gough and his lying friend. She may still have continued to see some of them. Take Shazia Singh with you. She seems to have a way of wiling things out of people.' He smiled wryly. It hadn't taken her long to winkle from him the hippie name his parents had foisted on him. It was something he did his best to keep quiet. Fortunately it shortened to a nice, normal, everyday sort of name. 'Maybe she'll get some interesting gossip from Chandra's friends. Anyway, just see what you can find out. While you're doing that, as the vicar is still missing, I'm going to see Dean Linklater's mother, see if she can tell us anything about Gough's usual hang-outs so I can check if he was at any of them at the time of the fire. After that, I'll see if his girlfriend's come back. Wish me luck. We could do with some firm answers one way or the other.'

'Maybe you should charge Gough anyway,' said Catt softly, only half joking. 'Look at the trouble it would save. Not to mention pleasing the Asian community and the brass PC brigade. Might even help me get my promotion.'

Casey's expression hardened. 'The day I do something because it's politically expedient and suits the "right on" causes is the day I'll pack the job in and go and become—' He broke off. He had been going to say 'become an old hippie like my parents'. Instead, he said quickly, 'Become a security guard'. Granted, Wayne Gough's an unpleasant individual, but is he the one who killed Chandra and the baby? He's going down for the other arsons for sure, they've got his thuggish signature all over them. But I want to be certain when I charge the killer that it's the *right* killer, whether they be white, brown or polka dot.

'God knows the liberal elite have compromised enough of the judicial system in this country. They've got half the police scared to even look at a non-white, never mind arrest them in case he's dragged in front of a disciplinary board. I tell you, ThomCatt, nobody's doing any spinning on this one, least of all me. I want the truth and I mean to get it, however unpalatable it might be in certain quarters. As the victims, Chandra and her baby deserve that much. They deserve justice. It's what the job's all about – or used to be.' He paused for breath and to regain his composure.

Catt stared in amazement at Casey's uncharacteristic outburst. However, he made no comment other than to observe, 'Better be damn sure then. If we arrest one of the ethnic minorities, especially one of Chandra's family, and it turns out you're wrong, you'll be crucified.'

Casey found a wry smile as he remembered his last Asian community meeting. 'Between the Asian community and the brass I'm likely to be torn in two long before anyone could do that. But if I'm not, you can have the words "I'm sorry. I made a mistake" carved on my gravestone after the crucifixion.'

'Amen to that.'

Casey arrived back at the station after speaking to Mrs Linklater to find that Catt had beaten him by five minutes.

'So, what did you find out?' Casey asked as they sat either side of his desk with the canteen's leftovers. The sandwiches had been made hours ago and were beginning to curl at the edges. Casey lifted a slice – the cheese was as sweaty as a prizefighter after ten rounds. Too hungry to care, he replaced the top slice and took a bite as he listened to what Catt had discovered.

'Only that Mark Farrell *did* want to get together with Chandra. According to her friends he had it bad. But – and it's an important but – he reads the papers. He's quite a bright lad by all accounts, and he knew that if he pushed it Chandra would take the consequences. Apparently he settled for friendship and made sure he rarely went to her flat unless he was part of a crowd.'

He had certainly gone at least twice in the past few weeks – and on his own, according to Angela Neerey, Casey thought. 'Hm. So you're saying the family can't have found out about them?'

'There wasn't, and never had been, anything for them *to* find out. There was nothing going on between Farrell and Chandra.'

'But did the family believe that? And don't forget the

unrequited passion on Farrell's part. It'll be interesting to learn if his alibi holds water. As you said, it's possible that his unrequited love could have pushed him into torching the flat on the principle that if he couldn't have her, no one else would.'

'But as it appears that they *weren't* having a thing, it at least seems less likely that the killings were done for "honourable" reasons. What about you? Find out anything more revealing about Wayne Gough than what he's already made blindingly obvious?'

Casey nodded. 'Dean's mum was surprisingly chatty now she's had time to recover from discovering that her little lad's an awfully big liar. She was relieved to know that Dean's not going down for the killings at least. And Gough's girlfriend has returned. Seems she needed to see her mother in London and discuss what she should do. Happily, her mother advised her to tell us the truth; all of it. By the way, you didn't tell me that Wayne's regular girlfriend is a surprisingly sensible, level-headed girl. She told me she's studying to become a social worker and—'

Catt snorted at that. He didn't have a high opinion of social workers. Casey wasn't altogether surprised the girl had turned sullen and unforthcoming when Catt interviewed her. 'What does she see in a moron like Wayne?'

Casey shrugged. 'Love's meant to be blind, like justice, isn't it?'

'It would have to be blind, bothered and stupid in this case. For a college student to fancy Wayne—'

'Tara Tompkins may be young, but she's sharp enough, Tom. She's also got Wayne's number. After I explained that her boyfriend would go down for a long time if found guilty of this fatal arson, she told me that Wayne's been an idiot. And *she* had been an idiot to let it go on so long. I think she's got plans to improve him – she struck me as the crusading type.' This brought another snort. 'She told me she'll change him.'

'The usual misguided claptrap, then. Do they never learn?'

'Perhaps she intends to use the study of Wayne for her thesis? Anyway, after a bit of umming and ahing and wondering if Wayne would forgive her for saving him from his macho self, she was far more forthcoming on the alibi front. She also enlightened me on how our Wayne came to claim the killings as his own in the first place. Apparently our two resident heroes had been boasting about the earlier arsons when one of their friends asked Gough if they'd torched "the Asian bird's gaff". Gough being Gough, said, "Yeah. We done that one, too. It was no big deal." He left Linklater no choice but to back him up or risk a beating for making Gough look a fool in front of his mates.' Casey paused, then added, 'Do you want to know where our errant vicar comes in? He turned up finally. I went to see him after I saw Dean's mother and Wayne's girlfriend.'

Catt raised neat, perfectly arched eyebrows – Casey was convinced he used tweezers on them – and said, 'Go on, surprise me.'

Casey gave one of his rare smiles. He couldn't help it. 'He was only at the local church. With the local vicar. Being questioned about his Christian virtues and promising to bring the kids up Church of England prior to getting married. Seems young Tara's an old-fashioned girl, and religious with it. She insisted on all the traditional trappings of marriage. God help her if her crusade's to turn Gough into decent husband and father material. Anyway, on the day of the Bansi arson, Gough was there for the service beforehand as well as the lecture on the sanctity of marriage, which the vicar gave them afterwards. They even took tea and cucumber sandwiches. He was there for the best part of two hours and didn't get away till after two p.m. so there's no way he could have set the fire.'

It was Catt's turn to smile. 'No wonder he preferred to go down for the killings rather than confess that lot to his mates.'

The strain the case had put them under showed as they met each other's eyes before collapsing in gales of laughter. The thought of the tattooed and shaven-headed Wayne Gough having to endure such unmacho indignities was too much.

As the tears coursed down his cheeks, Casey managed to gasp, 'He's already attended two services and lectures. He's got a third one waiting for him when he gets out of here,' before amusement choked off any more words.

It was the first, the only, bit of light relief they'd had since the case had started. Casey, for one, had felt as if a huge weight had been pressing him down. The laughter came as a welcome release.

Fourteen

M ark Farrell's alibi had checked out. Farrell, it became clear, was something of an entrepreneur and as he had said, he had been on a business trip to the Continent during the relevant time. Several of the business acquaintances he had met had vouched for him.

And as Casey headed wearily and unwillingly for home, after enduring another of Brown-Smith's PC homilies, he supposed he should be grateful that another suspect was now firmly removed from their list. The trouble was, of course, that all the eliminated suspects had been white. And in spite of his brave rhetoric to Catt about making sure justice was done, he was aware of the possible implications for his future career should the winding trail lead back to one of the super's less preferred suspects. And as, currently, Asians were the only ones remaining on the suspects list, that seemed only too likely.

He longed for some solitude and the return of his home to its previous peaceful austerity. His home had always been his haven, his retreat from the world and its problems. It was where he did most of his thinking. But since the outside world – in the shape of his parents – had taken up residence, he found himself increasingly reluctant to go home.

Instead, he had begun to work later and later, unwilling to face whatever further damage his parents had inflicted on his house. So far, between them they had put his hob out of action, stained and ripped his kitchen vinyl and damaged his sound system with their scratchy old sixties records.

Unfortunately, working late every night was turning out to be counterproductive. There was only so much information the human brain could absorb before it stopped functioning efficiently. Tiredness and the consequential irritability didn't help either. No doubt that was what had prompted his earlier outburst that had so surprised Catt.

He needed his quiet home back, his retreat. Only then would be begin to fire on all cylinders again. But there was little hope of that yet. His credit cards were up to their limit. He could of course increase the limits as the bank had so helpfully suggested but, after years spent sorting out his parents' financial muddles, he felt that was a slippery slope. He had never been keen on credit cards anyway, nor credit of any sort. The puritan in him felt that if you couldn't afford to pay cash you should do without. He'd only given in and applied for credit cards because they were so convenient, but he had strictly regulated his use of them. If he should start loosening his high standards now, who knew where he would end up? Confessing all to a meeting of Debtors Anonymous was a distinct possibility, given his family's propensity for addiction. And every addiction started with that one first step . . .

Casey reached home and put his key in his front door. At least he could get on his computer and do a bit of Internet research on India. With Gough, Linklater and Mark Farrell definitely out of the running, and no other possible white fire-setters on the horizon, it was time to dig a little deeper into the Asian community and their culture.

Just before he shut the front door behind him, he heard the sound of breaking glass from the living room.

What now? he wondered as he dumped his briefcase in the hall and called out, 'Who's breaking up the happy home?'

He had striven for lightness, but as he walked into his living room he couldn't help but wonder what else would need an expensive replacement or repair by the time his parents left. He soon found out.

'Hi, Willow, babe.' His mother smiled. 'What do you think? Looks good, hey?' She gestured behind her at the two fireplace alcoves.

This morning, they had held his cherished scripophily collection. Now, his glass-framed old share certificates, some with beautiful artwork, were stacked anyhow against the wall. No doubt that explained the breaking glass. In their place were his mother's Indian bazaar bargains, most of which had seen better days; assorted beads, his father's old sitar with its still-broken strings, and tatty old wall hangings, their once rich colours now sadly faded.

His austere but comfortable living room now bore more than a passing resemblance to an Eastern market. A very downmarket market. As well as most of their gear gradually spreading outwards from the spare room into his living room and the consequent mess and muddle, he was now expected to gaze admiringly at broken musical instruments and tatty old rugs.

On top of everything else it was too much and Casey opened his mouth to protest, but his mother forestalled him.

'I knew you wouldn't mind, hon. You *did* tell me to make myself at home and, as the Guru Manesh Yogi said, creating the right ambiance around oneself is *so* important.'

This from a woman who had lived over half her life with the pleasant ambiance of bailiffs hammering on the door.

'Besides, I found those symbols of capitalism you collect oppressive. Those railway ones gave me bad vibes every time I looked at them.'

Those two – The Stockton & Darlington and Liverpool & Manchester Railways – were only the most prized part of his collection. Two cherries on the cake, they were early nineteenth century, very rare and quite valuable. And as Casey leaned down to check the stack of frames, he was horrified to realize that the first of his prized cherries was the one with the broken glass. Quickly he checked the certificate for damage, all the while muttering under his breath.

'Do you know how many men died during the construction of those railways?' his mother asked.

As it happened, he did. He liked to learn about the historical backgrounds to the shares he bought. Though he doubted his mother could supply the answer to her own question. To Casey, his old shares were an interesting collection of social and industrial history, not a paean to capitalist worker exploitation, as his mother claimed. Some had become quite valuable since he had bought them. His favourites weren't even beautifully coloured like many of the foreign share certificates; old British shares tended to be on the plain side. It was probably why he liked them best of all.

He went in search of bubble wrap and brown paper, carefully removed the rest of the broken glass from the frame and wrapped it and its precious contents. He would have to get it repaired.

Perhaps he should put aside his qualms and get his credit raised on *all* of his cards. If he got that organized and could get the bailiffs to agree a cash payment, his parents might be back home as early as the end of the week. And he would have his haven restored. It couldn't come a moment too soon.

After dinner, no longer able to bear the squalor to which his previously austere but comfortable living room had been reduced, he took himself off to the boxroom where he kept his computer, switched on and logged on to the Internet. While the search engine was checking out likely sites, he made himself some tea and brought it back upstairs with him.

He checked the screen, glancing through the listings. Discounting the more obviously touristy sites, he quickly jotted down those he thought might be most informative. He took a gulp of tea and clicked on the first site.

Several hours later, his tea long since gone cold, he sat back, gazed at the pile of printouts and began a more thorough read through. He discovered that his mother and Shazia Singh hadn't exaggerated. Sati, or suttee, wasn't a thing of the past. According to his research there had been over forty *known* cases of voluntary or involuntary sati since India's independence in 1947.

One of the most recent cases was in Rajasthan – the young woman in her late teens whom his mother had mentioned. Her husband had died no more than seven months after their wedding. The young woman had been well educated by all accounts, and had apparently spent most of their brief married life with her parents rather than with her new in-laws. All the more strange then, that at the time of her husband's death, and briefly living with her in-laws, she had – according to them – elected to commit sati. The evidence as to whether this had been a voluntary act was conflicting. But what didn't seem in doubt was that, after being clad in bridal finery to meet with her young husband at the bridal altar in heaven, she had led the procession to the funeral pyre, been assisted aloft and burned to death.

Several witnesses had claimed the girl's sati was far from voluntary. In fact, getting an inkling of what was planned for her, the young woman had reportedly fled her in-laws' home and hidden herself in a barn. She had been found, dragged out, decked out in her bridal finery and led to her death surrounded by sword-brandishing youths. Witnesses said she had appeared drugged. Drugged or not, she had attempted to struggle from the pyre when it was lit, but had been weighed down by logs and coconuts, hemmed in by the youths. The fact that she was an educated young woman and from a well-to-do family hadn't saved her.

Nine years later, in 1996, all those accused of murder – of 'assisting' the young widow to commit sati – were acquitted. The case had caused a furore in India.

Casey read on and discovered one of the attractions of sati – for the widow's in-laws, if not for the widow. And now he remembered that Shazia Singh had also mentioned it. A woman committing sati, according to some Hindu beliefs, not only saved her husband's family and seven generations after the painful cycle of birth and death, it also guaranteed them entry to heaven. Some kind of guarantee, thought Casey. Some kind of motive for murder – if you were a believer. Even if you weren't, receiving an inheritance alone had proved sufficient motive for many murderers.

So far, apart from the house-to-house team checking out their alibis, Casey had spent little time on Chandra's in-laws. Even now, it seemed far-fetched to believe that such reasons would prompt them to murder, even given that in their grief they had blamed her for their son's death. Far more likely that they had baulked at Chandra inheriting her late husband's share of their business.

But they weren't alone in that. When it came to arguments – and violence – over inheritances, the British could teach the world a thing or two. Maybe, Casey thought, we don't produce social codes that required women to immolate themselves to save their honour, but we have our share of raping, pillaging and plundering invaders. The history of most countries produced a long, depressing catalogue of violence and grisly death. England had had forced marriages aplenty in earlier centuries. History books contained countless episodes of war, family feuds and murder over inheritances. Impossible, then, to adopt a high moral stance and condemn a practice begun from honourable motives during centuries long gone.

Yes, in these modern times sati did seem barbaric, but the First World had had a century or more of wealth and decades of widespread education to discover more sensitive modes of behaviour. India, like much of the Third World, was trying to drag itself from its feudal past, straight into the new technological world. What more natural, that in its struggle towards the twenty-first century some practises still lingered?

Even in India, a country heaving with assorted religious fervour, there had been scarcely more than forty cases of sati since independence, a drop in the ocean given the size of the population. It could hardly be said to be endemic. And India wasn't the only country where young brides suffered mother-in-law problems . . .

That reminded Casey. Rachel was due home from her tour at the weekend. He *must* ensure his parents had left by then. For a musician, Rachel was very clean living, very keen on order and, like Casey, abhorred clutter. Even though she had met them, she had no idea what his parents were really like. He'd made sure of that. Made sure, too, that his parents were on their best behaviour after issuing dire threats. He'd even demanded they stop calling him Willow for the occasion. He hated to be so censorious, but really, they gave him little choice.

He'd bought them new clothes; a conservative blue suit for his father, much to his disgust, and a subdued, grey silk dress for his mother. He'd even prevailed upon her to wear her wild bush of kinky, greying black hair in an elegant French plait. They had looked so different when he and Rachel arrived at the restaurant they'd booked for the occasion that he hadn't recognized them and had walked straight past their table. He'd had to be light on his feet to explain that one away. Families really were the very devil.

To his amazement Rachel and his parents had got on fine; even discovering a mutual admiration for some musician that Casey had never heard of. They'd had a ball. Well, everyone except Casey had had a ball. After days of anxiety about the occasion he'd ended up sulking and excluded from the conversation while the other three talked about musicians they had known, who they'd seen at festivals and in concert, and who was the greatest of all time.

Ironically, with his simmering sulks, *he'd* been the one who had caused shame and embarrassment. *He* the cause of the evening ending early. *He* the subject of reproachful glances and tart remarks. The unfairness of it, the supreme irony of it, took his breath away even now.

His gaze rested contemplatively on the screen and he realized he had got away from his research. Forcing his tired eyes and brain to concentrate, he read on, and learned that the majority of cases of sati seemed to have occurred in Rajasthan, the bulk around the Sikar district. He sat up straighter as it occurred to him that the 'drop in the ocean' suddenly appeared far larger, concentrated as it was to a particular area.

Casey realized that he didn't even know where in India the two families had come from. Maybe it was time he checked the backgrounds of Chandra's family, and her in-laws. It might be interesting to learn if either of them came from Rajasthan, which appeared to be the sati capital of India.

Too tired to concentrate any more, he shut down the computer and went to bed, if not to sleep. The vivid pictures brought on by reading about yet another young woman's agonising death churned on through a wakeful night. Mercifully, since Casey had finally got around to reminding his parents of the house rules, they weren't accompanied by overloud music.

When he got to work the next morning, Casey handed the pile of printouts to Catt and suggested he have a read.

'Reckon you're on to something?' Catt enquired.

'Don't know yet. Could be.'

Catt grinned. 'I know that look. Something's stirring.'

Something was, but it had yet to clearly reveal itself to Casey. It seemed that clarity required an extra input.

While Catt began to read the computer printouts, Casey got on to the passport office and asked them to check the birthplaces of the older members of the Khan and Bansi families and get back to him. He presumed by now they had all taken British citizenship. As for the grandparents, no doubt they held Indian passports. He would have to get on to the Indian high commission and hope the notorious Indian bureaucracy did not take too long to get through.

And while he had the services of Shazia Singh he might as well make use of them. Grabbing all the notes on the case, he went in search of her and thrust the paperwork at her, hoping that she would see something that his own culture blinded him to.

It only took her an hour to put her finger on at least one part of the evidence that had been niggling Casey. As she sat down in his visitor's chair and pointed out the relevant section, she said, 'See, sir. These red fibres and the jewellery round the body. Seems to me someone was trying to make Chandra a sacrificed bride.'

'Or trying to make it *look* that way,' Catt pointed out from his seat in the corner.

Shazia shrugged. 'Whichever. Presumably whoever did it, not being able to persuade Chandra that ritual suicide was a good thing, had done the next best thing and thrown the clothes and jewels over her so she would have the appearance of a widow dressed to meet her dead husband in heaven. You know, of course, that when Hindu widows were immolated in funeral pyres they were dressed as brides, not the widows they actually were?'

Casey nodded. 'I've been doing my homework,' he revealed. 'But as Sergeant Catt said, was this set-up done for religious reasons or to deliberately throw us off track?'

Shazia Singh shrugged. For once she had no answer.

More to the point, neither did Casey. But at least he was beginning to get a few ideas. He ushered both Shazia Singh and a protesting ThomCatt out of his office and shut himself up alone to think them through.

Fifteen

In spite of his splendid isolation and hours of thinking time during the day, when Casey reached home that evening he had still not managed to acquire clarity.

Casey's father, trying in his own way to be helpful, with a shaking hand offered him a half-smoked wacky baccy cigarette. Exhausted, drained, feeling beaten and with his mind elsewhere, unthinkingly, Casey took it and drew in a long, deep drag. Then another one.

It didn't take long for the drug to take effect. Soon he was as relaxed and laid-back as his parents. In his drug-induced, dreamlike state, Casey found himself travelling back over the investigation from a curiously high, godlike altitude, with a detachment that was equally godlike. He saw again the burned, blackened bodies; the charred floorboards at the centre of the fire; the threads of cloth and twisted metal that forensics had recovered. He saw the blue-skinned idol that had sat in the corner of Chandra's room. He even recalled its name. Krishna. *Hare Krishna, Hare Krishna, Hare Hare*, he muttered in singalong tones, to which his father's reedy voice companionably joined in.

He also remembered Shazia Singh telling him that Krishna held a special significance for widows. What was it again?

His mind went off at various tangents – Chandra – the manner of her death and that of her child – the idol in the corner that the neighbour didn't recall seeing – the first meeting with Rathi Khan and his family.

In the distant reality, beyond the suffusing, rosy glow of his

166

father's ultra-strong wacky baccy, Casey thought he heard someone knock at the door. He ignored it. Moments later, he became aware of his mother's voice, saying, 'Willow. Willow Tree, hon. There's someone to see you.'

Casey looked up to see Thomas Catt standing in the doorway, a bottle of wine in one hand, a bunch of flowers in the other and, on his face, an expression of open-mouthed astonishment as he sniffed the air and took in Casey's sprawled figure.

Casey waved him to a seat, wafting the wacky baccy's aroma towards him as he did so. 'Wondered when you'd turn up.'

ThomCatt, with his parental fixation, had a habit of latching on to the parents of others and practically adopting them. Once he'd learned that Casey's parents were visiting it had only been a matter of time before Thom turned up. Casey, imbued with love for his fellow man, couldn't understand why it should have bothered him.

'Willow Tree?' Wearing a bemused expression, Thomas Catt perched on the sofa beside Casey's now comatose father. 'I always thought you were a William.'

'That's what you were meant to think.' Somewhere, in the back of Casey's mind, anxiety stirred. But the anxiety was immediately swamped in a rosy euphoria and he sniggered. 'Willow Tree's the sort of name you get when you have hippies for parents,' he explained. He waved his arm again. 'Meet the folks – Star and Moon.'

Catt nodded politely towards Casey's mother, who immediately offered him a joint. Catt declined, equally politely. But a grin was starting to edge in on the corners of his mouth. 'I won't stop,' he said. 'I can see you're relaxing. I just thought I'd call on the off-chance that after shutting me out of the office you might have hit on something.'

'Hit on something?' Casey slurred. He sniggered again as he regarded the curling smoke from the wacky baccy. He'd hit on something all right.

'About the Chandra Bansi case.'

'Oh that. Thought I was getting somewhere a minute ago. Gone now.'

Catt stood up.

Casey stared up at the length of him. 'You going already? You just got here.'

'Just remembered I've got a date. I'll see you tomorrow. Don't get up,' he said to the three slumped figures, none of whom showed any signs of stirring. He held up the flowers and the wine and said, 'I'll just put these in the kitchen and let myself out.'

When Catt had gone, Casey took another puff, leaned back and a few minutes later the earlier, vague stirrings sharpened and he found the clarity of vision that had previously eluded him. Suddenly, like the kind of revelation about the secret of the universe that drug taking was supposed to induce, he saw everything sharply for the first time. He was surprised to find that now, as his inner mind was suffused with feelings of contentment and warmth towards all, the whole thing made sense. He wished Catt hadn't gone. He wanted to explain this marvellous clarity to him. Because he knew who had committed the double murder. He even knew why. The only thing he didn't know was whether he could prove it . . .

He gazed at the smouldering hand-rolled spliff and grinned inanely. Maybe he should have tried this earlier? Maybe it was time he gave up being the stuffed shirt his parents proclaimed him to be. Maybe . . .

The next morning Casey had trouble meeting his own eyes in the bathroom mirror as he shaved. He hoped Catt's arrival the previous evening had been a figment of his drugged imagination. But he suspected it wasn't.

Thinking of his sergeant reminded Casey of something Thom had said right at the beginning of the case. Catt had been inspired when he had said that whoever had done the killings must be either mad, bad or dangerous to know.

Casey wasn't sure whether it was the weed that had enabled him to stumble on the solution to the case. He hoped not, as he didn't want some devilish corner of his mind tempting him into a repetition the next time a case proved troublesome.

But he'd worry about any possible inherited addictive personality traits later. For now, he wondered how he could prove his conclusions – his father's wacky baccy wasn't *that* miraculous. He also wondered how he could explain his weak self-indulgence to Catt. After taking the moral high ground so often in the past on the drugs issue, he was conscious that the previous evening's exhibition made him look like a hypocrite. Catt would never believe it was his first smoke since his teens. He didn't want to lose his sergeant's respect. It meant too much to him.

After he climbed in the shower and took a long, vigorous scrub and shampoo to wash any lingering drug scent away, he was careful to dress in his most sombre suit from a wardrobe sombre with similar hues. Fortunately, the suit he selected had just come back from the cleaners. It was still encased in its protective plastic so was uncontaminated by telltale odours. It wouldn't do, after such a thorough scrub, to risk wearing yesterday's suit. Especially as he realized that the PC purgatory which had plagued him throughout the case was likely to be replaced by a hellish chorus as various combatants derided his conclusions.

Because, even though he was confident that he now knew the who and the how and even the *why* – if such a killing could have a reasonable *why* – he knew he had no proof worthy of the name. And if, as seemed likely, Chandra's family remained silent, his conclusions would receive a sorry reception.

He drove to the station through puddles of rain. The weather had changed overnight. The oppressive, sticky heat of the past week or so had finally gone, washed away by a heavy shower. Today was drizzly, grey and miserable and for bodies briefly acclimatized to sticky heat, the little breeze struck chill.

He picked up a grinning Catt at the station. For once, Catt had the good sense to keep his mouth shut and made no reference to the previous evening. Casey gave him a quick explanation of his conclusions on the investigation as they headed for the Khans' home. But when they got there the house was empty – truly so this time, Casey thought, as there was not even the telltale, swiftly withdrawn face at the window. There was an air of abandonment, even desolation, about the place.

'Perhaps they've flown the coop,' Catt suggested. 'Would be the best thing all round if they had. At least it would bolster your case.'

A week ago, Casey wouldn't have been tempted to agree with him. But he was tempted now. More than tempted to hope that Catt was right and that the hellish prospect waiting in the wings had flown out with them.

As they paused at the entrance to the drive for a break in the traffic, a middle-aged and expensively dressed white woman knocked on Casey's window. He lowered it and looked enquiringly at her.

'I've seen you on TV,' she confided. 'You're the officer investigating the death of Mr Khan's daughter. Were you looking for Mr and Mrs Khan?'

Casey nodded.

'Only they're all at the hospital. The old man was taken ill. He went off in an ambulance with Mr Khan. His wife and the rest of the family followed in the son's car.'

'When was this?'

The woman considered. 'Getting on for an hour ago. It's very sad. To think I saw Mrs Khan out with her grandson when I was walking the dog on the very day her daughter died. Poor woman, who would have thought that only an hour later she would suffer such a tragedy as to lose a daughter. And now this. They say tragedy comes in threes, don't they? I wonder what else they can expect?'

Casey didn't have to wonder. He knew.

'That family has certainly had more than their share of trouble lately. Why I remember—'

'I'm sorry,' Casey interrupted. 'But what was that about Mrs Khan?' His fuzzy brain had been trying without success to compose arguments to support his conclusions, and amongst all the woman's chatter Casey nearly missed what she had just told them. 'You saw her, you say, on the day of the murders? Why didn't you mention this to one of my officers when the house-to-house team questioned everyone in the neighbourhood?'

He threw a questioning glance at Catt, who could only shrug and shake his head. But the woman answered his question readily enough.

'I didn't tell them anything because I wasn't here. I left for the south of France for a short holiday the morning after it happened. Felt rather guilty, actually, to be sunning myself on a beach when the Khans had suffered such a tragedy. But it wasn't as if I knew anything that might help.'

Unfortunately, she *had* known something. It was information they could have done with much earlier in the investigation. Casey took a calming breath, belatedly noted her glowing tan and said, 'You mentioned seeing Mrs Rathi Khan on the day of her daughter's murder. What time was it exactly, and where?'

'Why?' The woman's eyes narrowed. 'Surely you don't think that she—?'

'Please, just answer the questions.'

The woman thought for a moment or two and then said, 'I saw her near that parade of shops on the corner of Ainsley Terrace. It must have been about twelve thirty, twelve forty-five. She seemed a bit distracted and didn't even acknowledge me when I said hello.'

Casey nodded, got Catt to note her details and thanked her. For a moment he thought that what the woman had told them would change everything, would turn his conclusions on their head. But then he realized that in addition to means and motive he now also had *opportunity*. The woman's information confirmed his suspicions rather than contradicted them.

Catt pulled a face once Casey's window was safely wound up and the woman had crossed in front of them and entered her drive. 'No flit then. Pity.'

Casey made no comment. He just asked Catt to ring St Luke's on his mobile to find out where they would find Rathi Khan's father and, presumably, the rest of the family, before they set off for the hospital.

To reach the hospital they had to pass The Lamb, and as Catt drove past Casey could see the weeping willows in the pub garden. Their boughs, previously held high and proud, were now heavy with moisture and the lower limbs drooped forlornly to the ground in a deep curtsey of dejection. Casey knew how they felt.

The Khan family were all sitting huddled in a corridor adjoining a side ward when Casey and Catt arrived. Apart from Mr Khan senior's wife, whom Casey glimpsed sitting by her sick husband's bed, the rest of the family were all together.

Casey belatedly realized that in his rush he had forgotten to pick up WPC Shazia Singh. But it was too late now to worry about such niceties. Instead, he sat companionably in a spare chair beside Rathi Khan and apologized for the bad timing. 'But I expect you can guess why we've come.'

Frozen-faced, Rathi Khan stared at him, then shook his head. His voice pitched higher than normal, he quickly denied it. 'I've no idea what you mean.' After a quick fiddle with his tie, which for once was not immaculate, he added, 'How could I have?'

So that was how he was going to play it. The acting was good but not in the Emmy class. In his spare time Casey had attended a course in body language. There he had learned of the various ways in which the body betrays the liar: the over-honest expression, the frank meeting of eyes, the pauses between sentences, the raised pitch of the voice, amongst others, were giveaways to Casey, even if he hadn't already learned most of them during myriad interviews with suspects.

Casey glanced at Catt and then at the other members of the family; Chandra's brother Devdan and sister Kamala, her mother, her sister-in-law, little Kedar and the other child. Each of the adults' faces was tight with apprehension and the determination to say nothing.

Before he could pose any further questions, a piercing scream broke the tension.

Casey leapt to his feet in alarm. Confused for a few brief, vital seconds, he was unable to locate the source of the scream. As he hesitated, Chandra's mother rose to her feet, her face a mask of horror, and pointed a shaky finger towards the glass screen around the side ward. She tried to speak, but although her mouth opened, nothing came out.

Casey turned, his glance followed the pointing finger. For a few moments, he too was frozen in horror at the sight that met his eyes. Then he leapt into action. Grabbing a conveniently situated fire extinguisher, he shouldered his way through the small crowd that had gathered and pushed open the door of the side ward. As he thrust aside the frantic but uselessly arm-waving student nurse, he banged down the plunger and aimed the thick stream of foam at the writhing figure on the bed. Its cloak of fire was almost immediately extinguished. All that was left was the pungent aroma of cooked flesh and a few lingering petrol fumes.

He felt the press of witnesses at his back and only became aware of the few seconds' eerie silence after a hysterical hubbub broke out. He closed his ears to the noise.

Neither body on the bed stirred. Although the brief but searing heat had fused the two bodies together in an eternal embrace, Casey was just able to recognize the two corpses – for corpses they were, in spite of his best efforts.

Rathi Khan's parents, Mr and Mrs Ranjit and Shrimati Khan, would now be together in paradise, just like Chandra and her husband. Or so the old lady had believed. How much of this was due to the growing dementia the family had been at pains to conceal, and how much to an unswerving religious belief, Casey didn't hazard to guess.

He stood aside as the 'crash' cart was wheeled into the room, swiftly followed by a second. Any attempt at resuscitation was likely to be hopeless, Casey thought. And so it proved, for after a futile ten minutes of exhaustive activity, the crash teams stood back.

It was only then that Casey became aware of the little boy's sobs just behind him. He turned. Kedar's eyes were huge and terrified, unshed tears clung to his lashes and he clutched his father's leg as though scared that he, too, was about to burst into flames.

'For God's sake, take that child out of here,' Casey commanded hoarsely. 'Do you want him to have nightmares for years?' He was too late, of course. Any damage to the little boy's psyche was already done. He had seen it all. Every horrifying second. Much like his great-grandmother must have witnessed similar scenes in her impressionable youth. Wasn't that what had brought all this tragedy about?

Abruptly shocked back to some semblance of normality, Dan Khan's gaze smouldered briefly, resentfully, at Casey before he turned and, without a word, strode from the room, lifting little Kedar into his arms as he went.

As though only the movement of one of their party could galvanize the rest, they all turned and followed, Mrs Rathi Khan and Kamala, her younger daughter – now her *first* as Rathi Khan had so indelicately phrased it – sobbing quietly. Only Rathi Khan looked back at the blackened bodies of his parents on the bed, then sighed heavily, shook his head, and followed the others out of the room.

It was some hours later. The two bodies were now safely enclosed in their metal shrouds in the mortuary. Both post-mortems had been speedily performed by a grim-faced Dr Merriman. There had been no surprises there, either. Mr

Khan senior had died from the effects of a second stroke that had followed on swiftly from the one that had put him in hospital. His death had prompted his Alzheimer-afflicted wife to commit sati. She had died from the effects of the fire. The slim flask of petrol she had concealed beneath her many shawls had been more than sufficient to ensure the flames took hold swiftly as she had thrown her flaming body on to what had to stand, in her damaged mind, for her husband's funeral pyre.

The other members of the family were finally willing to talk. After all, as Casey reminded himself, the murderer was now safe from any earthly retribution. He had discovered her guilt too late to save her from her sick mind. The old lady, Chandra's grandmother, wasn't mad or bad, not really. She was certainly sad and dangerous to know, though. Certainly for the widowed Chandra and her baby.

She was an old lady, already having her good days and her bad days when she arrived from India. Her son presumably hadn't been told that in her growing dementia, his mother had developed an unhealthy obsession with sati and might be dangerous.

As Casey sat in the living room which had become so familiar to him during the case, he wished he hadn't simply assumed that Mrs Khan senior's ill health had been *physical*. It would be as well for him to remember in future what dangerous things assumptions could be.

Now he asked Rathi Khan, 'So when was it you knew that your mother was responsible for the deaths of your daughter and granddaughter?'

Rathi Khan raised a pale and haggard face. 'I didn't know. Not for certain. But it would have been shortly after it happened. My son rang me at my High Street shop and told me my mother had been out and had come home with nasty burns on her hands and forearms.'

Casey nodded. When he had first spoken to them, directly after the deaths of Chandra and her baby, the old lady had been wearing long rubber gloves as he had remembered in the drug-induced clarity of the previous evening. He had thought nothing of it at the time as, upon their arrival, she had been engaged in the warmly domestic but dirty business of cleaning brasses.

'My wife told me that my mother had seemed exultant when she returned and kept on saying that Chandra was a goddess now. She immediately suspected what had happened. The dementia was getting worse all the time, harder to conceal. I believe the sati she witnessed in India in 1987 obsessed her, an obsession only compounded by reading about another well-publicized sati of a Dalit village woman in Uttar Pradesh in 1999.'

'Dalit?' Casey questioned.

'What were once called untouchables. They are no longer so, at least not officially, what with the government reserving places at colleges for them and so on; even in India, you see Inspector, change is possible.'

Casey nodded. 'Go on.'

'I believe those two prominent recent cases, together with the satis she witnessed or read about in her youth, must have deeply affected her.' His voice broke. 'The worse thing is that what she did she did out of love. The thought of Chandra suffering the usual unhappy fate of Hindu widows back home preyed on her mind. She really believed that Chandra would join her husband in paradise. She believed she would become a goddess.'

Rathi Khan gazed blankly at him, then said, 'But, of course, you know nothing of this.'

'Oh, but I do. Believe me, I do.' Casey turned to Mrs Khan. 'And what about you, Mrs Khan? Did you also suspect your mother-in-law had killed Chandra and the baby?'

She nodded. 'It soon became more than a suspicion.' Her English was suddenly surprisingly fluent. 'She actually told me what she had done and how she had done it as if she expected to receive praise for her actions. She thought I would be pleased, you see. Pleased that my beautiful Chandra had burned to dea—' Mrs Khan broke off on a sob. It was some moments before she was able to continue her explanation. After a juddering sigh, she continued. 'Normally, I never let my mother-in-law out of my sight. We were so afraid, you see, of what her obsession might lead her to do. She kept on and on about my Chandra being a widow and how she should now commit sati.' She broke off to explain, 'It's Sanskit and means virtuous woman or faithful wife. She tried to get her to pray and chant daily to Krishna, to shave her head and to smear her forehead with ash so as to mark herself as a disciple of Krishna, the protector of widows. She started referring to her as Mrs Dasi, the name adopted by widows who travel to Vrindavan, the City of Widows and the dwelling place of Krishna.'

Casey nodded. Now he remembered something that Govind Ghosh, Rathi Khan's assistant at the shop, had said. More to herself than to him, she had said that Chandra had died on Krishna's birthday; a day presumably chosen specially by her grandmother for its auspiciousness.

'That is why my husband moved Chandra and the baby to the flat. We didn't think my mother-in-law even *knew* about the flat, but she could be sly, you see.' She shot a reproachful glance at her husband. 'I said we should have locked her in her room so that I could get out, but my husband wouldn't hear of his mother being subjected to such treatment. He told me it was my duty as his wife to look after her and my father-in-law and to keep Chandra safe from her obsession.'

Her voice broke again. 'But it was impossible to watch her every minute. The day it happened, I was alone in the house with little Kedar and my mother-in-law. Devdan had dropped my father-in-law at the temple and gone off somewhere, and my daughter-in-law and the girls were shopping. Kedar was playing in the garden when he fell over. He gashed his arm badly. I couldn't stop the bleeding. Kedar wouldn't stop screaming. My mother-in-law was in our shrine room, praying to the gods, oblivious to it all, or so I believed. Usually she prays and chants for several hours at a time and I thought it was safe to slip out to take Kedar to our local chemist, who is a man of much skill. The shrine room has never had a key, but even if it had and I used it, my husband would never forgive me if he discovered I had locked his mother in.

'Obviously, it was impossible for me to take Kedar to the local casualty department – I didn't dare leave my mother-in-law alone for the time that would take. Even so, I was gone no more than twenty, thirty minutes, but when I returned she was nowhere to be found.'

A sudden torrent of tears gushed from her eyes, streaking her cheeks with kohl. 'I was frantic. What was I to do?' she appealed to them. 'I was alone in the house with Kedar and . . . and . . .'

'You had no choice,' Casey reassured her. He glanced at her husband. 'I'm sure we all appreciate that. Please go on.'

Mrs Khan took another shuddering breath. 'When she returned she had burns on her hands and scorch marks on her clothes. At first all she would say to me was that Chandra was happy now. Happy in paradise with her husband. But she was so ecstatic about what she had done that she told me all about it. How she had helped herself to the spare key to Chandra's flat and let herself in. She told me Chandra was in the bathroom and little Leela was in her cot, screaming. She had plenty of time to splash the petrol she had brought with her around the room. Imagine what my daughter must have felt when she came out of the bathroom and discovered her grandmother between her and the baby and caught the reek of petrol. She must have immediately guessed what was in store for her.' Mrs Khan's eyes were bleak with the thought of her daughter's terror and suffering. 'I couldn't contact Rathi, so I rang Devdan on his mobile and he rushed over here.'

Her words revealed that he had been told another lie; so where had Dan Khan been when it was claimed he had been at home? Wherever it was, as Casey glanced obliquely at the tight, unhappy face of Rani, Devdan's wife, it was clear she had her suspicions about where he had been.

'By then, my mother-in-law had told me the rest. That she had given Chandra the choice as to whether she struck the match immediately and engulfed them all, or let Chandra go to her child and give her a strong sedative so she wouldn't suffer. She seemed surprisingly rational when she told me all this. She was more in charge of herself than I've seen her in some time. She boasted of how clever she had been. She said she made sure to keep well out of Chandra's way as she crossed the room to the baby so she wouldn't have time to rush my mother-in-law before the match was struck. But Chandra wouldn't have risked that. I know my daughter, Inspector. She knowingly sacrificed her own life when she must have been aware she had a chance to save it so she could spare her child enduring the torment Chandra knew she was about to suffer.'

During the several seconds' silence that followed Mrs Khan's appalling revelations they all had time to imagine Chandra's horror. Casey, for one, was relieved when Mrs Khan again took up her story; it helped a little to mask the dreadful images in his mind.

'Rathi had arrived in his High Street shop by the time Devdan got here. For some reason he was concerned that the call might be traced and thought it better to ring the shop from a public phone. He went out to do so and told his father what his mother had done.'

Casey nodded. He already knew that important phone call had been made from a public phone box. He had thought it odd at the time. Now he knew the reason for it. He turned back to Rathi Khan. 'And that's when you rushed from the shop?'

'Yes. I ran first to Chandra's flat, saw the flames shooting from it and watched the firemen as they worked. I listened to the crowd outside, hoping desperately that she and the baby had been rescued in time. But, according to the onlookers, the fire crews found both Chandra and Leela dead when they arrived.' His voice cracked as he added, 'Both burned beyond recognition.' He paused, gulped in several deep breaths before he flatly added, 'I came back here then and we thought of what we should say. My mother was subdued by then, I knew I could shortly expect a visit from the police, so I set her to cleaning the brasses. I have found that giving her a simple practical task calms her mind, gives an element of normality. The rubber gloves also concealed her burned hands. Her face was only a little bit burned at the side and a shawl soon covered that.'

Casey nodded. No wonder, with painfully burned hands, her brass cleaning had been so desultory. But a lifetime of doing her duty, of pleasing her menfolk, had brought ready acceptance of a task that would cause her pain.

Mrs Khan broke in. 'We're missing a vacuum flask. And my mother-in-law's favourite Krishna image is gone from the shrine room.'

Casey nodded and asked what colour was the flask.

'It was red.'

The flask discarded amongst the rubbish bags in the alley behind Chandra's flat had been red. It had reeked of petrol and there had in fact still been some petrol in the bottom. They had had no luck in tracing it to its source as it was at least ten years old, made by the thousand and sold up and down the country.

'Do you know what she told me when she returned?' Mrs Khan's haunted eyes met Casey's. 'In her demented state, she was so pleased with what she had done that she wanted me to share her joy. She told me she had insisted that Chandra chant to Lord Krishna before her immolation. And Chandra, no doubt desperate to give the drugs she had fed the baby time to work, was forced to join in this macabre ritual as she waited to die. I can hear her voice all the time in my head. *Hare Krishna. Hare Krishna. Hare Krishna*, till I think I shall go mad.'

'Your daughter was a very courageous young woman, Mrs

Khan,' was all the consolation he could offer her. 'Try to force
your mind to concentrate on that. She died bravely, with
honour. It is something to be proud of.' He paused, unwilling
to ask Mrs Khan to endure the pain of further explanations.
But there was one other aspect of Chandra and Leela's deaths
he wished to clarify, and it wasn't as if Mrs Khan would ever
be able to escape the tortuous pictures in her own mind. Casey
doubted he would be able to either. 'Our forensic experts
found jewellery scattered around your daughter's body and
the remains of expensive fabrics. I presume they were Chandra's bridal finery?'

Mrs Khan nodded. 'My mother-in-law had brought Chandra's wedding sari with her. And although she didn't attempt
to persuade Chandra to wear it or the jewellery, she got as
close to the traditional ritual as she could. She told me she
threw it all over her as she lay dying.'

Casey glanced at Rathi Khan in the heavy silence that had
fallen. Perhaps he read reproach in Casey's glance, for Casey
had no chance to say anything before Rathi Khan launched
into a torrent of impassioned speech.

'What was I to do, Inspector? Remember this was my
mother we're talking about. She had Alzheimer's. She wasn't
responsible for her actions any more than Chandra's little
daughter would have been. When Magan, Chandra's husband, died she began to tell Chandra that she must become
sati. At first Chandra laughed about it. We all did. But then
my mother began collecting chunks of wood and coconut hair
and built a pyre in the back garden. Suddenly it wasn't so
funny. She took Chandra's bridal sari and hid it so that it
would be ready for the day, she said. She sounded so sane, so
matter of fact, that it was frightening.

'By this time we were all terrified of what she would do, so I
got the tenants out of the flat and moved Chandra and the
baby in. We didn't think my mother even knew about the flat,
but she still had her lucid moments and must have taken in
more than I thought. I certainly never imagined she would be

able to get herself over there on her own.' Head in hands, he added brokenly, 'I thought Chandra would be safe there. I thought what I did, everything I did, was for the best. I didn't know what else to do. My brother in India refused to have her back. He couldn't bear the stigma. He had never been her favourite son.' He gazed plaintively at Casey and asked, 'What happens now? I suppose we'll be charged as some sort of accessory?'

Casey hesitated. Personally, he thought the family had suffered enough. 'As to charges, I'll need to discuss that with my superintendent, but I think I can safely say he's likely to take a lenient view. But it would at least stop all the hotheads from trying to stir up trouble if you'd all come down to the station and make statements. Get everything out in the open.'

Rathi Khan nodded. 'We'll come. Of course we'll come. We would not like all these sad deaths in our family to be the cause of any further tragedy.'

Evidently believing that the day's revelations released him from his vow of silence, Catt remarked, 'I'm surprised you didn't try to arrange to get your mother back to India, safely secreted in some out-of-the-way village where we'd never trace her.'

'I was trying to, with my brother's help. But he wasn't being very co-operative. I wasn't thinking clearly enough to talk him round. What with the shock of Chandra and Leela's deaths – and at the hands of my own mother. Then my father's stroke . . .' Rathi Khan raised his gaze to Casey's. 'You may not believe this, Inspector, but I loved my daughter. She was the apple of my eye. But I loved my mother, also. Always I have tried to be a dutiful son. Chandra and Leela were dead – my mother was still alive. Naturally, I had to protect her.' He sighed. 'I believed the marriage I arranged for Chandra would be a good one, with a man I knew already adored her. Many women –' briefly his gaze rested on his plain, sad-eyed and neglected daughter-in-law sitting alone in the corner of the room – 'would be thankful for such a loving husband. I knew Roop Bansi, Chandra's mother-in-law, could be difficult, but I was sure that in a few short years Chandra's husband would be persuaded to move away from his parents' home and find a place of their own. He was ambitious and had far more drive than his father. He had the modern ideas, too, just like my son. And like my children, he had been born and brought up here. More English than the English – isn't that what you say?' He essayed a tiny smile that quickly faded. 'Things are changing in our community. The old ways are giving way to the new. It is right that they should. But for Chandra things didn't happen quickly enough.' His shoulders sagged and all at once his face took on the furrows and contours of a much older man. Faintly, he added, 'I am not such a fool as to make the same mistakes with my second daughter.' He stood up. 'Please give us a few minutes and we will come to the station and make those statements.'

Casey and Catt waited in the hallway while the family gathered themselves and their grief together. 'Terrible business,' a subdued Catt muttered as they waited. 'Not only his mother, daughter and her child gone up in smoke, but I imagine his reputation, too.'

'Maybe we'll all be pleasantly surprised,' said Casey. 'Sometimes tragedy brings out the best in people. We'll just have to wait and see. But at least the super and the rest of the PC brass will have to accept the outcome. Maybe now they'll stop their eternal hand-wringing and apologizing and start realizing that not everything white is bad and not everything black or brown is good.'

Catt snorted. 'I wouldn't bet on it. Last I heard from one of my Asian snouts was that the not-so-super has arranged to don saffron robes and join in a procession with the Hare Krishna lot down the High Street.' Catt shook his head in disbelief. 'Why, for God's sake, can't he be what he is – white, middle-class and Christian – instead of always aping the rituals of other faiths? To my mind, a man who won't stand up for his own beliefs or people is unlikely to be a reliable defender of anyone else's either. Not a very healthy thing in a senior police officer.'

Casey could think of nothing to add to that. Shortly after, they formed their own procession as one, two, three cars followed one another in almost funereal mode to the police station.

And as the family signed their statements, Casey could only hope it put an end to all the hatred. At least till the next time.

Sixteen

'Do any of us really know who we are?' asked Catt much later. The Khan family had long since left and he and Casey were about to leave for home themselves. 'Did Chandra? Caught between two worlds as she was, how could she ever find the time to discover her true self?'

Making the first – and Casey hoped the last – reference to the other evening when Catt had turned up at his home, Catt added with the sharp insight Casey had come to recognize, 'Do you? You whose whole lifestyle, it seems to me – apart from what I presume was a lapse the other evening – has been deliberately chosen in reaction against your parents' way of life.'

Catt's words prompted Casey into an evaluation of himself as he climbed into his car and drove home. Had he became who he was merely in reaction to his parents' hippie lifestyle? Rather than because it was what he *wanted* to be? Casey felt Catt might have a point, to an extent at least. But unlike poor, beautiful, tragic Chandra and her child, he had a chance to do something about it. He had a chance to metamorphose into the true him, whatever that was. But maybe it was time he found out what it *might* be.

Maybe it was time he tried doing some of the things he should have done in his youth, might have done in his youth but for his parents continuing to do them in his stead. Wasn't that meant to be the whole point of youth? To discover who, what, you were? Like Chandra Bansi, he had missed out on all that. Chandra had tried to accommodate her family's demands, while he had been too busy acting the responsible parent to ever really have a youth himself. Maybe if he now, belatedly, went through the rituals of the young, he would come out the other side a more rounded individual.

Official communication with the Indian authorities had revealed that Rathi Khan's mother's mental health had been failing for some time before she travelled to England. Presumably the culture shock upon her arrival in modern Britain had furthered the extent of the disease. Her son had told them that, until her marriage at the age of thirteen, his mother had lived all of her life in one village – Sikar. Like all Indian brides, on marriage she had moved to her in-laws' home village. As a child she had witnessed widows committing – or being forced to commit – sati. Didn't they say that the memories and experiences of youth were the ones most vividly retained as one grew older and began to lose one's grasp on reality?

Chandra's parents had, in some ways, been rigidly old-fashioned. So, by clinging to their hippie lifestyle long after its glory days had passed, were his parents. Strange he had never realized that before. And to think they accused *him* of being a stick-in-the-mud reactionary.

Maybe, as well as finding the true Willow Tree Casey, he ought to persevere with changing his parents, dragging them into the twenty-first century, rather than them thinking he should adopt the fading mores of a generation that had never been his in the first place. And as he opened his front door and shouted, 'I'm home,' he reflected that, truly, this case had opened his eyes to a lot of things.

Poor Rathi Khan. What a predicament he had found himself in. His daughter and granddaughter murdered, yet he had been unable to give himself over to grieving; this natural emotion had had to be put aside in order to protect their murderer, his own mother.

Casey was conscious of a sudden chill along his spine as he realized how easily any individual might find themselves in

such a position. With, at first, a few barely noticed alterations
in behaviour, the subtle chemical changes in the brain could
bring who knew what obsessions to stalk the mind of one's
daily companions.

And as his parents packed up around him, preparing to
return to their smallholding in the morning – rather than raise
his credit card limits he had made the ultimate sacrifice of
selling his most treasured share certificates to clear his parents' debts – Casey thought about how dementia might affect
them.

Rathi Khan's mother had become obsessed with the sati
rituals she had witnessed in her youth in Sikar, memories
strengthened by witnessing the 1987 sati episode in Deorala in
Rajasthan, when she was already showing the first signs of
dementia. Maybe she had also read about the Dalit woman
who committed sati in the nineties.

Casey, horrified at what effect such dementia could have on
a family, uneasily considered his own. What might his family
and friends' individual obsessions push them into doing? His
parents, for instance? How many times had he read that drug
use, particularly of the variety and extent that his parents had
gone in for, induced psychotic episodes? Schizophrenia, for
instance, was believed by many medical experts to be a direct
consequence of drug taking.

And as his father picked up the guitar that had been a
constant companion for decades, fondled it and started a
tuneless strumming prior to packing it away in their assorted
baggage, Casey studied him for signs of incipient madness.
Athough his father looked much the same as he always had,
so had Rathi Khan's mother. Just because a person looked
normal – or relatively normal in his father's case – proved
nothing. How dreadfully ironic that such catastrophic
changes should be so invisible.

His father, if so affected, might become convinced he was
the greatest guitar player the world had never heard, and
would probably, if he could summon sufficient energy, merely

take up harmless, if singularly untuneful, busking; demanding money with a menacing tin ear and tambourine accompaniment.

His mother, whom he caught with the corner of his eye hunting through his father's discarded jeans for his wacky baccy pouch, would perhaps, with her innate curiosity about everything, take up serial snooping or stalking.

Catt, of course, would surely develop an unhealthy obsession with other people's parents, while Rachel might well murder her orchestral conductor. How often had she voiced the desire to kill the maestro currently behaving like a megalomaniac during rehearsals? Perhaps with the bow of the first violin – another daily irritant – specially sharpened for the deed.

As for himself, maybe his dotage would encourage him to take up the irresponsible hippie lifestyle he had spurned as a youth.

That left Superintendent Brown-Smith. But, on the whole, Casey thought he would really prefer not to dwell on the prospect of the PC obsessed super going quietly, invisibly demented while still in harness. After so much tragedy such thoughts really were the stuff of nightmares.